# PATH OF THE CHIEF

# PATH OF THE CHIEF

*Ed Blanchard*

Writer's Showcase
New York  Lincoln  Shanghai

# Path Of The Chief

Writer's Showcase
an imprint of iUniverse, Inc.

For information address:
iUniverse, Inc.
2021 Pine Lake Road, Suite 100
Lincoln, NE 68512
www.iuniverse.com

ISBN: 0-595-26025-X

Printed in the United States of America

*For Lucille Hazel for bestowing upon me a love for
the written word and Bonita Margaret for
unfailingly encouraging me to try my hand.*

# CHAPTER 1

*T*he deer lifted its head and Fortier froze in place. It was a large buck whose savory meat would be a welcome change from the fish he had consumed in the swamp for the past two days. He held his breath for he had no intention of letting the buck escape. He could not see his Opelousa partner, but he knew that the Indian had not drawn the deer's attention. He realized that his own movements must have disturbed the deer and he silently cursed himself. Gabriel Fortier feared he had been too long out of the wilderness.

For the past two months, he had been away from New Orleans and its surrounding wetlands. The river ride he had taken on the trading vessel to St. Louis had been interesting and he had not been disappointed at its difference to New Orleans. He had enjoyed the company of the dark Spaniards that spoke of blue mountains to the west that Fortier had never seen.

The only harsh memory from his holiday was that of the barrel-chested trapper that had been away from spirits too long. Had Fortier not been drinking himself, the altercation most likely would not have taken place. The trapper had commented on Fortier's below average height. The Frenchman had been chatting with a frontier girl, and the lady had challenged him with her eyes.

Her eyes had said, "Well little Frenchman, what can you do against this monster from the mountains?"

Fortier's vanity had made him answer. It was obvious to onlookers that the trapper had the advantage of strength over the Frenchman. But, as the pair grappled, it also became obvious that the trapper, in his drunken stupor, had underestimated the Frenchman for Fortier had quickly knocked the larger man to the floor. Not wishing to waste this advantage, he then kicked the trapper in the groin and went home to New Orleans.

Fortier never took unnecessary risks. He could think of nothing in his life that he knew of that would give him reason to risk maiming or anything worse. Certainly not his own pride. He had been alone and on his own since his youth, and he did not wish to be responsible for anything other than his own well being.

The deer returned to grazing and Fortier released a soundless sigh of relief. The edge of the forest in which he lay concealed ran a hundred meters or so to his left and then became prairie. The buck stood fifty meters from the large white oak that the Opelousa intended to shoot from. Fortier estimated that his partner should be near the spot when he saw the buck's small tail rise. The sound of the shot reached him and he saw the deer take a step forward and topple.

Fortier was thinking of the Indians uncommon accuracy with the old musket when he saw him step from the trees.

The skinning and butchering of the deer was cheerful business for two men hungry for venison. The Opelousa and Fortier rarely spoke and they were both eating their second deer steak when Fortier said, "Good shot." The Indian seldom acknowledged Fortier's comments so he decided to try for conversation again.

"How long have you had that old musket?"

"It was for my father," replied the Opelousa.

"Tipak Tipak," The Frenchman struggled to pronounce a word and then said, "Three weeks we have been together and I still cannot pronounce your name."

The Indians only response was a shrug.

"What does it translate to in French?"

The Opelousa paused a moment before answering and then said, "I have not asked what your name translates to in my language. We are partners and we trust each other; that is enough."

The Opelousa stopped eating abruptly and turned to look into the dense forest. He stared for a moment and then continued his meal. Fortier noticed his concentrated listening and said,

"Do you expect to encounter someone hereabout?"

"Atakapa war parties come raiding here from the west," the Indian answered.

A discomfort settled over Fortier for he had never ventured past the great basin that ran from the large gulf, south of where he sat, halfway to the post of Natchitoches, far to the north. Of course he had heard the usual stories of the fierce Atakapa that inhabited this region, and their rumored cannibalistic practices, but he was certainly not prepared to confront them.

"I have heard that Atakapa lands are west of here. We have not reached the bayou where the elephant was found, and their land is beyond that."

The Opelousa sat stoically, munching his venison. Fortier knew that his partner was not one to fear shadows. Perhaps they should turn back east or strike north for Natchitoches.

"Can we avoid Atakapa hunting grounds and still reach our destination?" the Frenchman asked.

The Opelousa seemed pained to answer for something else had drawn his attention to the forest. After a long moment he said,

"As I told you before, yes we should avoid enemies, but the Atakapa roam where they please."

"In that case," Fortier said, "Just as I insisted we stay here and enjoy this venison, I insist you relax and forget about these Atakapa."

The Opelousa turned to Fortier.

"Not so long ago, the Atakapa sent runners to New Orleans to ask for traders to visit their land. They told your leader that they would settle in permanent villages like the other tribes if the traders came.

They offered to stop their wandering and stop raiding. Your leader did not accept their offer. He thought them too lazy to be of any profit. He told them the trade route was too long. This did not please the Atakapa chiefs. I would think that visitors will not be welcome in or near Atakapa lands for a while."

Fortier knew then that he should not have gone directly into the wilderness upon his return to New Orleans. It would have taken a while for the news of this insult to the Atakapa to reach him, for this was certainly small news in New Orleans, but vital out here.

"I wish you would have told me this before we set out," Fortier complained.

"I am surprised you did not know this," the Opelousa answered, "I know of all that happens in my tribe, I thought you knew of what happens in yours."

"You know how large New Orleans is," Fortier countered angrily, "how many hundreds of people live there. Do you suppose I could know of everything that occurs there?"

Fortier slumped into a crouch, throwing his unfinished meal aside.

"You know little of white men," the Frenchman mumbled.

"My father was one," the Opelousa stated with a grin.

Fortier was astonished and stared at the half-breed for a moment before he spoke.

"So that explains the near perfect French you speak."

"In a way," the Opelousa answered, "I never knew this courier-du-bois that sired me, but he taught his tongue to my mother. She taught me because there were so many Cannouche coming into this land. She said he was a good man."

It was a dark and quiet night. As they settled for sleep, Fortier noticed that the Indian kept his musket in his hands when he curled into his blanket. The Frenchman decided to choke down his apprehension and decide on what he would do in the morning. He seated himself on a log for the first watch and decided that the mosquitoes were not as bad tonight as the previous night.

"What happened to your father?" Fortier asked quietly.

"The Atakapa killed him," mumbled the Opelousa.

Nementou had first seen the deer when it had been startled from its grazing. He silently cursed himself for having disturbed the animal. When he saw the deer return to feeding, he decided to close the gap between himself and the buck. He had taken his first step when the shot rang out. He saw the deer fall as he molded himself to the ground. He had no doubt that it was either a Cannouche or an Opelousa that had fired the shot.

He did not wish to encounter any white men for he was apprehensive and mystified by their weapons. He was a bit disgusted that these Cannouche had refused to trade for his furs and tallow but he did not understand any of their actions before this refusal anyway. He knew that some Opelousa possessed fire sticks and hoped that this may be one that had felled the deer. His hatred of the Opelousa was his strongest emotion and he felt a perverse pride in it.

Nementou's grandfather had been killed by an Opelousa war club on the little hills when the three tribes of cowards had joined against his people. His father had taken the deadly pebble from an Opelousa firestick one winter past and had taken a long time to die.

Nementou's village never mourned the old ones. They would have felt foolish mourning his father for he had lived a long and fruitful life and had gone to the place above in a glorious fashion. Regardless of this custom, Nementou could not forget his father. He longed for his wisdom and patience. Suddenly he felt a fresh pang of bitter remorse and decided to find out if this was some wandering Opelousa. He would send his spirit to the shades and hang his body for the crows. His squirrel bark beckoned his companions.

From off to his left came Chaoui's answer. Nementou's brother was three years his junior and one of the most capable warriors in the village. Since a boy, Chaoui had mastered the use of his knife, and his bow was as much a part of his body as the bamboo shoots that adorned his chest. Nementou suspected that Chaoui felt no intense hatred for the Opelousa for he knew that his younger brother had not condoned his killing of two lost Opelousa children, months earlier. Nementou could see much of his father's wisdom in Chaoui, but not when it concerned Opelousa.

Chaoui and two other warriors soundlessly approached Nementou and blended themselves into the foliage. The four Ishak lay without a sound until dusk fell. When the night creatures began to stir, Chaoui whispered to his brother.

"Is it a Cannouche?"

"Too quiet for a Cannouche," Nementou answered.

"I smell deer meat on the air," Chaoui said, "an Opelousa would be gone from his place of killing."

Darkness descended quickly in the thick forest. After a long period of silence, Nementou spoke again; his voice filled with venom. "The Opelousa fools adopt the ways of the white men more every day. They give their women to the Cannouche for fire sticks."

After another long pause, Nementou continued.

"Take Ouaron and approach them from the large palmettos on our right. We will wait until the first light of morning."

"And if it is a Cannouche?" Chaoui asked tentatively.

Nementou grinned for he had known this question would come from his younger brother.

"We will ask him if his chief has decided to trade with us."

Twigs cracked as Chaoui moved away and Nementou at once became angry. By making sounds, he knew that Chaoui was being careless. It was as if Chaoui wanted the hunter to know of their presence and flee. No matter, Nementou thought, Opelousa or Cannouche will not hear Chaoui. He settled into a comfortable position and sniffed the roasting venison on the breeze while waiting for dawn. He thought of his dead father all night

Fortier slept fitfully for a while and it seemed only a few moments had passed when his partner was shaking him. He came awake with a start that made the Opelousa grin. He thought for a while of how to make his proposal, and then decided to simply say what was on his mind.

"I think we should turn north."

The Opelousas' face told Fortier nothing so he continued.

"There is no reason to take chances with these Atakapa when we can hire ourselves to the fort at Natchitoches as hunters. It will be much easier than trapping and dodging Atakapa war parties at the same time. We can try our luck in the southwest some other time."

The Opelousa turned his full attention to Fortier and studied him as if he had not seen him before. He took a long time to reply.

"My friend, the Atakapa are said to eat the flesh of their enemies, but they are still only men. I will not run from rumors and campfire stories."

"What are you saying?" Fortier exclaimed.

"I am saying," the Opelousa said patiently, "that I am wary of the dangers in the wilderness, but not afraid of them."

"Well," Fortier said, "I think it is foolish to venture into a place in which we may end up being killed or worst, and your trapping ground to the southwest is that place. I am turning north for Natchitoches."

The Opelousa never took his eyes from Fortier the whole time the Frenchman spoke. Fortier realized that this was the first time he had ever gotten the Indian's undivided attention.

"Caution is a wise thing," the Opelousa finally said, "for in this land it may keep a man alive; but an overcautious and timid man should not be in this land."

"You may go to the devil," Fortier shouted, feeling shame burn his cheeks from the Opelousas' words. "We part company here."

The Frenchman stooped to gather his belongings and he heard thunking sounds and a grunt from the Opelousa behind him. He turned and witnessed his partner collapse to the ground with three arrows protruding from his back.

The Frenchman scrambled for his musket as screams pierced the air. As he took up the weapon he felt a hard blow to the back of his head and he was enveloped by darkness.

When Fortier awoke he was sure it had been a dream. He was tied to a tree and the same big trapper from St. Louis was squatting before him, staring into his eyes. All at once he realized that it was no dream and certainly not the trapper. As the haze began to clear he saw two Indians raising the body of the Opelousa into the lower branches of a cottonwood. His partner was quite dead. His upper torso had been horribly mutilated and his face was a bloody pulp. The two savages elevating the body muttered to one another and their low chuckles sickened Fortier.

Surprisingly, the Frenchman also felt a hint of anger. He had always considered himself friendless and the Opelousa had been a fine partner. He knew that he must concentrate on escape immediately and forget the hapless Opelousa, but the sound of the laughter disrupted his thoughts.

He turned his attention to the Indian directing the hanging of the body. The tall warrior seemed to relish the desecration of the corpse. Finally, he could not help but return the stare of the slim brave squatting before him. As he toyed with a knife, his eyes never left Fortier's face. The Frenchman could detect a form of innocent intelligence in his eyes, but his knife quickly became Fortier's focal point. He wanted to ask if they understood French but decided against it; most of all, he wanted to be away from here.

Fortier knew that this horrible Atakapa animal was probably trying to determine what kind of meal he would make and the Frenchman began to mumble to himself.

'Pray to God,' he stuttered, "that the cannibal stories were only rumors."

Chaoui turned from staring at the white man and spoke to his brother.

"Nementou, he is awake. He is speaking to his spirits, or to himself."

Nementou walked to the tree that held the white man and looked hard at his injury. He would have killed this one for being in the company of an Opelousa, but before their attack he had overheard what seemed to be an argument between the two.

Perhaps he should have waited for the argument to escalate; the white man may have killed the Opelousa for him. No, he knew that he was meant to kill the Opelousa the moment he had seen him. He would use the white man as a slave. He would give him to Soco for she needed help to compensate for her age.

"Do you know any of his words?" Nementou asked of Chaoui.

"No, they all roll into one sound, but Kata will understand."

"I will give this Cannouche to Soco," Nementou said. "She will remember how to handle a white slave and she needs help. Kata is frail and when you give her a child it will be hard for Soco."

"You are wise and good, my brother," Chaoui said with a smile.

The misty look that Chaoui could never understand came into Nementou's eyes when he spoke again.

"I will never have the wisdom of our father. I try to fashion myself after him and yet I cannot succeed. He would not have killed this Opelousa. He would have given him some of his smoked fish for the Opelousa' knife, but he would not have killed him. I really think he liked the Opelousa, even though he could not trust them."

"He trusted them," Chaoui said. "There were few things he did not trust. He trusted the alligator to come up from its hole when he hunted it, the oysters to fill his baskets and yes, the Opelousa, to trade with him in time of peace and try to kill him in time of war. And of course he trusted you, Nementou. To replace him as Chief when he went above."

Nementou looked with deep affection at his brother.

"Chaoui, you should have been our fathers first born."

The younger man laughed and raised his voice so that the other two braves could hear when he spoke.

"Come, let us sing tonight of our success while we feast. I know you all long for your women after this hunt, and I yearn for my Kata. Come, let us take this gift to Soco."

Fortier was certain that these four braves had decided to include the rest of the tribe in their feast. He guessed that the slim savage had decided he had enough meat on him to feed more than four.

As they began their walk, he appraised his captors. Their appearance was not unlike any other Indians he had seen up and down the great river. All four had splendid physiques and one was rather tall. They were dark skinned and their black hair was cut short and coarse. One of them had extraordinarily large ears. He was undoubtedly the ugliest human being Fortier had ever seen. Ha! Some human beings! Taking him to some primitive cooking pot.

An unusual feature he noticed on all of them was the piece of cane inserted through their nipples. One of the four had only one nipple impaled this way, but the other three had both teats sporting a length of bamboo. He could not imagine what strange culture had brought about this practice.

They moved through the forest at a brisk pace for what seemed to Fortier at least four or five kilometers. At mid-day they came to a large bayou much wider than the streams they had thus far forded. The Indians uncovered two pirogues from the reeds that contained additional weapons, a large bundle of skins and a cache of dried meat. Until now, they had been traveling due west. Entering the bayou, their direction became southwest.

Fortier had been placed between the two braves that faintly resembled one another and he soon detected a powerful stench being emitted by them both. He decided that they were after all quite dif-

ferent from the tribes along the great river with whom he was familiar.

Well on their way, the Frenchman wondered why the Indians had
not taken his weapons. One of the chuckling warriors had shown
some interest in his musket, but the tall warrior had insisted it be left
behind. If the tall brave was the leader of this band, he was indeed a
foolish one. Fortier settled in the craft and tried conjuring a method
of escape.

Hours later it seemed they had been traveling for days. Cramped
down in the bottom of the narrow pirogue, Fortier had become most
uncomfortable. They had paddled, according to the Frenchman's
estimation, steadily southwest.

The white man began to ponder his predicament and cursed himself for having argued with the Opelousa. He knew that if he had not
captured the Opelousas' full attention and spoiled his acuteness to
the danger, they might have had some warning of the attack. The
Opelousa had been wrong to trust him. He was an inexperienced
fool that was responsible for the death of his comrade. Now the
Opelousa had joined his father in the portion of Heaven reserved for
Atakapa murder victims.

Morbidly, Fortier realized that at least now the Opelousa would
finally know his father, and unless he himself did not fabricate some
escape plan immediately, he would know the Opelousa' father also.

In spite of the jeopardy of the situation, Fortier could not help but
appreciate the beauty of the land they were traveling. On each side of
the bayou was dense woodland, but occasionally, prairies stretching
out to vast distances could be glimpsed just beyond the trees.

The forest was comprised of numerous oak, cottonwood, hickory
and cypress trees. There was an abundance of wildlife and Fortier
could see why these Indians were said to inhabit the forest rather
than the stretching plains that only contained the seasonal buffalo.

When Fortier was ready to scream from the nagging pain in his
lower back, the Indians stopped and pulled to the bank. The French-

man could see that the bayou was cluttered by a wash-up of fallen trees just ahead. Gladly relieved to stand, Fortier helped the Indians carry the pirogue around the obstruction. He noticed his two captors glance curiously at one another and he again felt shame numb his cheeks. He supposed they had expected an escape attempt rather than help.

As the paddling continued, Fortier dozed sporadically. He was brought fully awake by the sound of voices an undetermined time later. Ahead he could see a rather large village on the bank of the bayou. It was growing late and the whole population of the village must have been turned out, for he could distinguish men, women and children present.

The two pirogues turned toward the village and Fortier reasoned that this must be home for his captors. Drawing closer, the Frenchman estimated a population of fifty or sixty. The men were all adorned as his captors, and the women wore deerskin and moss.

As the boats pulled to the bank, some of the people ambled over and spoke to the paddlers. When they noticed Fortier's white face peering up at them from the middle of the pirogue, they all began to scream. It was more or less heavy grunts from the men, but the women wailed as if in pain. Fortier was so terrified by this that he feared he might swoon. These were not people, they were monsters.

The tall Indian climbed from the pirogue and walked away from the bayou with two of the villagers. The Frenchman did not move as his other three captors remained in position in the boats. He could not help but notice that all of the Indians milling about the pirogues had the same peculiar odor as his captors. He sank as low as possible into the bottom of the craft and prayed silently to himself that these people had already done with their supper.

# CHAPTER 2

---

❀

*T*his village was in fact not the home of Nementou and his hunting party, but that of Kinimo. This chief and his band were neighbors of the hunters and the stop was made only to enable Nementou a few boasts of his accomplishment in capturing the white man.

Kinimo greeted Nementou with a look of indifference. Nementou ignored this and attributed Kinimo's actions to jealousy for he was certain the chief had heard the women's screams indicating a captive.

"Greetings fellow chief," Nementou said. "My companions and I have stopped for a moment to exchange news."

Kinimo's indifferent voice matched his earlier expression when he spoke.

"I was informed that your hunt was successful; are white men your enemy now as well as the Opelousa?"

The insult clearly angered Nementou and his smile of greeting left his face. He knew that Kinimo, like Chaoui, did not approve of his killing of Opelousa for the neighboring chief's grandmother had been of that tribe.

"Kinimo," Nementou said quietly, "my father trusted and respected the Opelousa and it earned him his death. Be wary of where you spread your affections."

The expression on Nementou's face and the edge to his words joggled Kinimo's manner and he spoke in a different tone.

"Forgive me, my words were harsh and your father was a noble man."

Kinimo directed Nementou to a seat inside of his large hut and took on a more social manner,

"What have you learned in your forage?" he asked.

Nementou's temper had cooled somewhat and although he did not feel conversational, he knew that to receive any news he must offer some.

"More Cannouche traders are coming into our land," he said. "Some of them are offering firesticks for furs. They ask many furs for a single firestick and a handful of the powder that it needs. They cheat us but I fear many of our people will still trade with them. I for one will not allow this form of weapon in my village."

"But why, Nementou?" Kinimo exclaimed. "The fire sticks are more accurate than any of my warriors arrows."

Nementou ignored the remark he was tempted to make about Kinimo's warriors and replied innocently.

"Any bowman can release five arrows accurately in the time the firestick explodes once."

"I will not prevent my people from obtaining them," Kinimo said. "They make us equal to the white man."

"Most of our people feel the same as you," Nementou admitted. "Enough of this talk of weapons; what information can you offer me?"

Nementou's neighbor leaned in close and spoke in a whisper.

"The powerful shaman Lacassine visited us not long ago. He still hates the whites as you hate the Opelousa, and he tries to persuade everyone he visits to think as he does."

Nementou speculated for a moment and then answered.

"Lacassine is a powerful shaman, for he fears no chief and it is said he collects the dead."

"Your white captive," Kinimo inquired, "What are your plans for him?"

Nementou smiled and looked thoughtful before he spoke.

"He will bring some excitement to our village for a while. He will help the women, fish with the children, and I suppose someday I will send him on his way."

The two Chiefs then walked to the bayou together. Nementou was happy he had stopped for now news of his captive would spread. The neighbors wished good fortune and as the visitors pushed off into the bayou, Kinimo called after them.

"Be aware, Nementou. If Lacassine learns of your captive, he will surely kill him."

Fortier estimated that they had only been gone from the village of screamers for an hour or so when another village was sighted. He was sure now that this was the village of his captors for still a long way from the huts, many of the Indians on the bank began shouting and waving to the pirogues. The faces of the warriors that had captured him remained impassive as they approached the village, but Fortier noticed the taller Indian's chest puff a bit when he disembarked the boat.

The majority of the villagers stared at the Frenchman curiously. The second Indian from Fortier's pirogue jumped to the shore and embraced a young woman.

The tall, sturdy warrior moved to the center of the assembled villagers and began an oratory that Fortier knew must be brag of how he had returned with many spoils, including a white fool. The Frenchman was grateful that none of these savages had gone through the screaming ritual and hoped that their silence did not indicate hunger.

The tall Indian concluded his speech and practically all of the villagers stood nodding with approval to whatever he had said. Fortier was led to the center of the group of huts and fastened to a stout red pole jutting from the ground there. From a hut near this pole emerged a wrinkled, crooked person whose gender Fortier could not discern. The ancient creature shuffled over to the captive without any of the hesitance or timidity all of the other tribe members had shown toward him. Drawing near, Fortier decided it was probably a woman because of her garb, the deer skin around her waist that was the same texture as her skin. She looked directly into the Frenchman's eyes and spoke.

"French?"

"Yes, yes my good woman," the elated Fortier burst out. "I am French. I have come to plot a trade route for my people and I was captured by your brave warriors. I am sure it was a simple mistake, for I am certainly no enemy of your people. I would like…"

Fortier stopped speaking when he noticed the old woman's eyes. He had been saying anything that came to his mind that might save him when he realized that the old woman had understood nothing that he had said. He decided to try his words again and more slowly. Before he could say anything, the old woman leaned close to him and sniffed him strongly. She began to laugh, turned and walked away. Her retreating cackle dismayed Fortier as much as her horrid sniffing had. When Fortier found himself praying that he would give them all indigestion, he knew that he must be losing his mind.

Chaoui enjoyed watching Kata move inside of the hut. He was confident that the meal she was preparing would be flavorful, in spite of his unexpected return, for his Kata was a good woman. She set smoked fish, slivers of squash and persimmons before him and sat to watch him eat.

"Are you happy I have returned?" inquired Chaoui.

"As much as I was unhappy when you left," she answered with a smile. The smile left the girl's face when she spoke again.

"Chaoui, why a white man?"

"Nementou does what he thinks is best for himself and the village," Chaoui answered. "You must not question his decisions."

"I would not question him outside of this hut," the girl answered.

"He will not harm this Cannouche," Chaoui said. "He feels that by bringing a captive to the village, the people will approve of him."

"The white man was alone?" Kata asked.

"An Opelousa was with him," Chaoui answered quietly. Kata knew what this meant and said no more. She busied herself about the hut, appearing to desire no further information from her husband.

"Will you speak to this white man?" Chaoui asked.

"Are you certain he is a Cannouche?" returned Kata.

"He is Cannouche," said Soco as she entered the hut. "I said one of their words to him and he began chattering like a squirrel."

"His fear will make Nementou more powerful," said Chaoui.

"His fear will be drowned by misery tonight," laughed Soco, "His skin is untreated, the mosquitoes will drain him."

"I suggest that you care for him, Soco," Chaoul said, "Nementou intends to make the white man a gift to you until he is set free."

"Bah!" answered the old woman. "I have had one white captive in my life and that is enough. He shared my hut, ate from my field, taught his strange words to my little Kata and then was gone! We should give this one to the Karankawa's."

"Mother," Kata admonished, "Cako was a good man. He became as noble a warrior as any in the village."

"You speak of him more than you speak of your dead father," Soco squawked to her daughter.

Kata approached the old woman, caressed her gently and whispered.

"As you do, Mother."

"Bah!" croaked the old woman as she left the hut.

Kata turned and noticed Chaoui smiling, and when their eyes met they both laughed aloud.

"And what does the brother of our Chief wish for me to tell our white prize?" asked Kata.

"Tell him his duties, and that no harm will come to him if he does not attempt escape," Chaoui said still laughing. "Tell him he is the honored guest of Nementou, Chief of the Vermilion Band of the Hiye Kiti Ishak."

Kata sat beside Chaoui and embraced him intimately and whispered,

"You are my chief, Chaoui."

"You may speak to the white man in the morning," Chaoui mumbled as he pulled his wife to him.

The village was beginning to stir when Fortier awoke. He had slept only in short intervals during the night for the mosquitoes had eaten him alive, and even now practically covered him. None of the savages seemed bothered by the infernal insects and the Frenchman speculated that they were probably immune.

The Frenchman saw the wrinkled old woman coming towards him holding a bark container. He was still on the ground, bound to the tall red pole. As the old woman bent and offered him the bowl, Fortier found it to be some form of gruel and he realized that he was famished. The last food he had consumed had been the venison and that seemed to the Frenchman ages ago.

He looked at the old woman and spat his words at her.

"You wish to fatten me up, eh? Well, I cannot eat very well with my hands tied, you old devil."

"If you wish to eat, your hands will be unbound," Kata said, joining the old woman at the pole.

The French words made Fortier whip his head around to the speaker. He saw that it was the young woman that had embraced one of his captors previously. He was shocked, but he spoke quickly.

"You know French! Yes, yes, I wish to eat. I would also like to know why I am a prisoner."

"I will answer your questions if I can," said Kata. "I have been told to speak to you first and I will do this after you have eaten."

The Frenchman was puzzled as to how this woman knew his language, but his deliberation did not last long. He wolfed down the gruel while staring at the young woman. She was pretty, in a primitive sort of way. Her hair was long and braided in places and she wore a tanned deerskin from waist to knees. Her breasts were concealed by moss that passed beneath her arms and was bound behind her back.

Fortier was swallowing the last mouthful of gruel when the Indian girl spoke again.

"Where were you going when you were taken?"

Fortier saw no reason to lie. The fabricated tale he had blurted the day before had been a result of fear. Although the fear was still present, he had gained enough self-control to think clearly.

"We had wished to trap the streams and marsh southwest of here. We did not know your people are so hostile to strangers."

"We are not hostile to strangers," the girl answered. "Our chief has a blood oath against Opelousa, and they are no strangers. I must also ask that you speak more slowly, for I have not spoken your tongue for a long time."

She was certainly no master of the French language, but Fortier was grateful that he could at least understand her.

"You will be released soon and given work to do here in the encampment," the girl said. "You will not be harmed in any manner unless you try to escape."

"Are you people Atakapa?" Fortier asked, as the girl started for her hut.

"Others call us that; we are the Vermilion Band of the Ishak.

"What are you called?" Fortier asked.

"I am called Kata," the girl answered shyly, moving away from the Frenchman.

"I am pleased to meet you, Kata. I am Gabriel Fortier, recently of New Orleans. How long will I be kept here?"

The young woman moved away without answering. As Fortier considered the circumstances, he knew that his chance of reaching a civilized place on his own was almost non-existent. The poorest Indian tracker would catch him before he reached Natchitoches or anywhere else.

When he considered what the girl had told him, he felt the fear of his predicament subside a little. Escape was out of the question and rescue was highly improbable; but if he followed this wandering band of savages, as all Atakapa were said to do, they might come upon a white settlement to which he would then escape. Perhaps his fortune was not so bleak after all.

# CHAPTER 3

*T*he village of the Vermilion Band of the Ishak was not large. Fortier estimated a population of thirty-five. Eleven of this number was braves, the rest women and children. Eight weeks had passed since his capture and his existence had become routine. He was no longer bound to the red pole at night, and he was free to roam the boundaries of the camp when not engaged in labor. His duties of helping the women tend their corn and melons did not burden or embarrass him and he had felt a sense of achievement when he was given a bone tipped spear to accompany the village boys to fish.

His captors had also started sending him into the forest alone for firewood. At first he had suspected that this did not indicate trust, but rather indifference to whether or not he escaped. But whenever he did not complete a task properly, he was severely reprimanded and he began to realize that they did depend on him for his share of the work assigned.

Fortier was also sure that his capture had been a result of Nementou's vanity. He had detected hints of the Chief's insecurity as a leader from his long conversations with Kata and he suspected he had been taken to prove to the village that Nementou was worthy of filling his dead father's position.

Since his capture the village had moved a half days walk north. The site was a small bluff near a well-stocked bayou lined with trees full of small orange-red fruit that the Indians called plaquemine.

Fortier was busy fashioning a new hut for his family. He had never had feelings for anyone the way he had developed feelings for Kata, Chaoui and Soco. His relationship with all of them was closer to a family unit than he had ever had, and it had grown dear to him quickly.

Chaoui was patient with him and after a short period of time, had stopped treating him as a half-wit child. He had taught him much of the Ishak ways, using the hand sign language common amongst the tribes along the great river.

Kata seemed endlessly happy in his presence, always wanting to hear more of his stories and descriptions of life in New Orleans among the French.

Soco, although habitually bad natured, was at first tolerant and then kind to the Frenchman as he learned more of what was expected of him.

Occasionally Fortier found himself resentful of the attention Kata heaped upon Chaoui, but it was usually fleeting because of Chaoui's kindness. The lithe young warrior had taught Fortier how to fish, how to oil his body with the alligator oil whose pungent odor repelled insects as well as a host of other valuable things that the Frenchman knew he would not have been able to survive without.

Fortier was placing hides on the roof of the new hut when he saw Kata approaching with a basket of oyster shells that would be their fireplace.

"The hut is strong, Chaoui has taught you well," the young woman said.

"I owe Chaoui much, but teaching me to build a hut was to your advantage. Now you do not have to build them," Fortier laughed.

"He likes you, Hiyen," Kata said with a smile. "He teaches you as he would a little brother."

"Kata, why do you call me that?" Fortier asked. "Is Fortier so hard to say?"

"It is such a heavy word," the girl answered. "And you are much like the Hiyen."

Fortier felt a smile overcome his seriousness. He found he could never become angry at the girl's innocence for she was incapable of insult.

"I would have enjoyed knowing a white woman of your honest innocence, Kata," Fortier allowed, "but I still do not like to be called opossum."

The girl smiled and started into the hut. She stopped and stepped back to look up to the roof at Fortier and the Frenchman noticed a serious look about her face.

"When the village is settled," Kata said quietly, "Chaoui and I will go to the lake of sacrifice. He has told me to tell you that he wishes you to accompany us."

"What is this about?" Fortier asked.

"My husband and I go to make offerings of prayer to the spirits so I may have a child."

"What is the reason for my presence?" Fortier asked.

"For three nights Chaoui must climb one of the hills around the lake of sacrifice and call to the spirits for a child," Kata said. "He trusts that you will protect us while he prays."

Fortier was touched. He had seldom known trust and he knew now that he was no longer a captive, but one of them. He was elated by this sense of belonging. He jumped to the ground from the hut roof smiling.

"Why do you smile?" Kata asked, "This is a serious thing we request of you, Hiyen."

"I am just happy," Fortier said. "And Kata, tell Chaoui that I like him also."

As the Frenchman began to gather the remaining hides, the girl stood staring at him.

"You are a strange man, Hiyen," she said as if to herself.

Fortier stopped and addressed the girl.

"You do not understand, Kata. You see, when I was a child...I mean to say that it has never been easy for me to..."

As the Frenchman spoke he saw Kata's puzzled look deepen.

"It doesn't matter that you do not understand. Perhaps it is better if you do not understand. You see, your way of life is so different from mine. You are all so primitive and yet trusting and non-deceitful."

"Hiyen, please do not think that none of the Ishak are evil, for I assure you some are."

Fortier continued as if he had not heard the girl, "I suppose it is my way of life that has formed my character that I so dislike and has earned me the name, Hiyen. For the first time in my life though, I trust and care for someone, Kata. You and Chaoui and Soco also,"

The girl shook her head and asked, "Does all of this mean you will accompany us?"

"Tell Chaoui," Fortier said eloquently, "that I will be honored to accompany you and I will protect you both with my life."

The girl laughed and walked away leaving Fortier whistling with merriment at his newfound conviction.

The Frenchman started to return to his work and noticed an elderly Indian man squatting next to a tree a short distance from the new hut. He had noticed the old warrior on a few occasions, but had never given him any thought. What arrested Fortier's attention now was the fact that the old man was staring intently at him and appeared to be in deep thought.

"Kata, one moment please," Fortier called after the girl.

Walking briskly to the entrance of the hut, Fortier spoke while trying to keep his glance averted from the ancient warrior.

"Who is the old man that sits near our hut?"

"He is called Yok."

"I am curious, I only notice him occasionally; is he a member of this village?"

"In a way he is," Kata said. "He lives alone near our village. He is not considered one of our group, but he is always near. When we move, he follows."

The girl started away but the Frenchman persisted.

"Don't you wonder why?"

"If there is a reason, it is his," Kata said.

"Is it common for him to sit and stare as he is now?" Fortier asked as Kata started to move into the hut.

"Oh Hiyen!" the girl exclaimed as she stopped and stepped back from the hut entrance.

"You are so full of questions always. Yok is a harmless old man that chooses to live away from the village. Some say the spirits once touched him and that he is sacred; others say he was once a chief that proved to be a coward and was banished from his band. None of us know for sure for most of our old ones are gone to the place above. It does not matter, Yok is helpful. He asks nothing from the village and yet he brings meat and salt to us. He supplied Soco and I with all of our meat before we moved to this band and Chaoui's hut."

"Soco!" Fortier said, "she is an old one. She would know about Yok."

"Soco never speaks of him. I have heard her speak to him on a few occasions and all she did was call him a fool."

"And yet he would still bring you meat?" Fortier asked with a laugh.

"Perhaps the story about him being touched by the spirits is the one to believe," Kata said, smiling as she entered the hut.

Fortier chuckled and turned to where the old man had squatted. He was gone.

The day of departure for the lake of sacrifice was drawing closer and Fortier had vowed to himself that he would prove his dependability and trustworthiness on the trip. Although his evenings were often occupied by conversations with Kata about New Orleans and what she called the 'white world', he seldom if ever felt remorse about being away from there. The Frenchman enjoyed watching the looks of excitement and wonder from Kata when he spoke of churches, schools and hospital. He had even added embellishments to his stories of adventure and heroism on the riverboats that plied the great river, for the sole purpose of receiving nods of satisfaction from Chaoui after Kata translated his tales.

Proving himself to the village would earn him a place of respect amongst the warriors, and he could finally be considered one of them. He often daydreamed of having his own woman, living in his own hut in the same fashion as Chaoui and Kata. He wondered what Nementou and Chaoui's reaction would be to such a concept. He was sure that they would both say that to live in his own hut, he would have to earn the privilege. This 'earning' practice of the Ishak was not one of his favorites at first, but he had learned to appreciate the satisfaction derived from accomplished objectives.

His fantasizing about a woman and hut of his own had been cut short by his present predicament. He had been sent with two of the village boys to dig for clams on the white reef that was just visible from the shore of the great water. The waters of the gulf had been placid when they had crossed them earlier that morning. After filling three baskets with the succulent clams, the trio had noticed thunder-heads rolling rapidly toward them from the south. Immediately they had struck for the large bay that was their ingress to the gulf, and they had hoped that this bay would provide them adequate protection from the increasing winds. The bay washed upon a long stretch of marshland that turned into prairie a few kilometers from the shore. If they could at least reach the coastal marsh, the worst of the danger would be behind them.

As Fortier and the two boys paddled steadily in rhythm, the rain began to fall. After a spattering of large, cold drops, it fell on them in torrents. Fortier peered into the driving rain and could just see the outline of the nearing shore. He could barely hear the excited chatter of the boys over the wind and rain. A strong gust from the squall seemed to blast them from the right side of the pirogue and the craft overturned. To Fortier, it seemed the boys were catapulted into the air. The Frenchman felt panic envelop him an instant after he was plummeted into the warm waters of the gulf. Surfacing, he pulled frantically for where he thought the shore to be. He could see nothing and his mind screamed in confusion. All conscious thought left him as he mechanically continued to stroke. He felt searing pain in his lungs as an occasional breath pulled in a small amount of the heavy brine. His arms felt weighted with lead and his vision became nonexistent, whether from the storm or from exhaustion, he could not discern. When he felt the first wave of unconsciousness accost him, his fingers dragged mud. The wind helped to propel him up onto the muddy shore, and he lay for a long time gasping for breath in the subsiding storm.

As quickly as the storm had raged out of the gulf, it was gone. When Fortier regained full consciousness, he stood and watched the squall speed north over the prairie. He immediately began walking along the shore, searching for some evidence of the boys. His calls were whipped away by the last vestiges of the wind. After two hours of walking east and west along the shoreline and finding no trace of the children, he collapsed against a clump of driftwood into a nightmare-riddled sleep.

Katash was having trouble keeping up with the pace being set by Chaoui. They had left the village just after daybreak and it seemed to Katash that they had been running ever since. After the two village boys and the white man had not returned the evening before, Chaoui had volunteered to go in search of them. Choc, the father of the two boys, had pleaded with Nementou to be allowed to accompany Chaoui, but Nementou had chosen Katash because he excelled at tracking. He did not excel at running though, and he struggled to stay with Chaoui.

"Chaoui," Katash wheezed, "You run as if you know where we are going. I cannot look for sign at this pace, we must slow down."

"We will begin at the place that we hide our fishing pirogue," Chaoui said. "If the pirogue is there, they are between the coast and the village. If it is not there, they faced the storm on the great water."

The two warriors trudged along, nearing the end of the prairie. Their going was slowed by the soupy condition of even the prairie land, made so by the heavy rain dumped by the storm.

"Could the white man have let the storm catch him on the white reef?" Katash asked.

"I hope that I have taught him better than that." Chaoui mumbled.

The usual paths through the marsh had all but been obliterated by the strong winds, and the sun had passed its zenith before the runners reached the coast. It was difficult to discern the hiding place of the fishing pirogue in the aftermath of the storm, but Katash found it. Most of the reeds and grass had been blown away, but the indentation of the craft in the shore was still present. Chaoui and Katash stood staring, as if mesmerized, at the evidence of the absent pirogue for a long time. Katash started the first notes of the death song, but Chaoui waved him to silence.

"I will start along the shore to the east, you go to the west," Chaoui instructed. "We will meet back at this place at sunset."

Chaoui started along the shore, praying silently to himself. He had gone no more than one hundred paces when he heard Katash's shouts. He turned and ran back in the direction from which he had come. Rounding a bend in the shore, he saw Katash waving his arms, standing above a seated figure. Approaching, he recognized a mud-splattered Hiyen, staring out over the water, seemingly oblivious to their presence.

Crouching before the Frenchman, Chaoui spoke gently while accompanying his words with the sign language.

"Hiyen, where are the children?"

The white man continued to stare as if he had not heard or seen. Chaoui took hold of his shoulders and shook him roughly. When eye contact was made between the two, Chaoui repeated his question.

"Hiyen, where are the boys?"

"The wind caught us in the bay," Fortier whispered hoarsely.

"I do not know your words," Chaoui signed. "Use the sign language."

Fortier signed that the pirogue had been overturned by the wind and that he had been able to swim to shore.

"Could you not save either of the boys?" Chaoui signed.

Fortier shook his head with tears glistening on his cheeks. Chaoui turned away from the white man in embarrassment.

"This white man is a woman," Katash exhorted. "He weeps because he did not try to save the children as a warrior would have."

"That is enough, Katash," Chaoui said, "We were not there and we do not know what happened. We will return to the village and let our Chief hear what Hiyen has to say. He will decide what must be done about this."

As the two braves and the Frenchman started back to the village, Katash voiced what was already in Chaoui's mind.

"It is fortunate for the white man that Nementou did not allow Choc to accompany you, Chaoui. It would not have been easy for you to stop Choc from killing this white man here on the shore."

Once again in his life, Fortier felt he was in the wrong place. His earliest childhood memories were often fleeting because they were usually harsh. The woman that had cared for him from infancy had taught him to survive any way he could on the New Orleans riverfront. He had never been sure of her age or whether or not she was his relation. She insisted that he call her Monique, and that she was not his mother; but her acquaintances called him "her boy." Those acquaintances were the rough keel boatmen from upriver that visited the river city as often as the rains.

He had known he was in the wrong place in Monique's cottage when he was around ten years old. The latest boatman "acquaintance" had drawn him aside one evening and told him that he should run away from the cottage and not return. In fact, he had made it plain that if Fortier did not, he would never run anywhere again. So he had left that semi-secure existence and pragmatically applied Monique's survival training on the levee among the French and American traders.

After several years of near starvation as a street urchin in the young but rapidly growing city, he had become a keel boatman himself. The keelboats had shown him a little of the world beyond New Orleans. Just enough in fact for him to know that something other than barge labor was his calling. The winding, muddy river had given him glimpses of vast, mysterious lands that beckoned to him.

He apprenticed himself to an old trapper that stalked the marshes south of New Orleans and had learned the trade quickly under the tutelage of the elderly man. But Fortier did not have fond memories of the old trapper, for even after he was fully trained, the old man would not give him partner status. He felt Fortier was indebted to him for his instruction and would only give him meager wages.

The marshes south of New Orleans had become the "wrong place" for Fortier when the old man had introduced him to the Opelousa. Fortier had quickly taken advantage of the fact that the Opelousa had no partner in trapping and left the ungrateful old man.

Before he and the Opelousa had set out he had decided to treat himself to a brief holiday in St. Louis. That northern town had been a "wrong place" for him because of the burly mountain man; he and the Opelousa had ventured into a "wrong place" that led to his capture, and now he was in another "wrong place."

"As Fortier, Chaoui and Katash approached the village, the Frenchman reproached himself for not having left this place long ago. He knew that Chaoui was grossly disappointed in him for not having tried to save the two boys. Didn't Chaoui realize that all that would have accomplished was his own loss of life?

Kata had tried explaining the codes of honor and pride that the village warriors practiced but he had thought them foolish and had paid little attention. He had no idea what his punishment might be for Chaoui would not answer any of his inquiries. There had been no communication for the entire return trip from the great water.

Chaoui noticed anxious faces peering at them from inside huts and around cookfires as they walked into the village. As he expected, his brother stood waiting for him at the base of the red ceremonial pole. Approaching Nementou, Chaoui heard the wailing song of mourning emanating from Choc's hut.

"The white man and the children were blown over by the wind on the great water," Chaoui announced to his brother and the village. "The white man alone survived."

A chorus of angry shouts and weeping bellowed from all corners of the village. A furious Choc rushed to Nementou and loudly spit words filled with venom.

"This white man is evil, as are all white men. I have heard the great shaman, Lacassine. This devil has spirited away my sons and he must be punished."

Nementou rapped his staff of office against the ceremonial pole to quiet the uproar that followed Choc's words. When a semblance of calm descended, the chief spoke.

"This matter will be decided at a council of decision. We will meet when darkness has fallen."

The Chief turned and walked to his hut. Murmurs of debate could be heard throughout the village compound. Fortier walked to his family's hut and sat outside the entrance. Kata rushed to his side with tears of concern glistening in her eyes. Chaoui moved past them, into the hut, without a glance. As he passed, he mumbled harshly to Kata, and Fortier saw the girl grimace at his words.

"What did Chaoui say?" the Frenchman asked anxiously.

"He said that if you leave the village he will track you and kill you."

# CHAPTER 4

When night was upon the village and the council convened, the eleven warriors of the Vermilion Band filed stoically into the council hut. Only proven warriors of the village were allowed to attend a council of decision so Fortier had no choice but to wait for the outcome seated outside of Chaoui's hut.

Chaoui was the last of the warriors to find his seat in the council hut, for since Nementou's calling of the meeting, Kata had sat with him pleading Hiyen's innocence. As he took his seat in the hut, he prayed silently that the position he intended to take was the correct one.

"Who wishes to speak on this matter?" Nementou called from his position before the assembled warriors.

As expected by everyone present, Choc rose quickly and spoke with passion.

"Not long ago, my woman and I visited with her father and mother, who as you all know, are of the Calcasieu Band that live near the lake of brine. While we were there, a shaman known as Lacassine addressed the village about a danger that threatens the way of life of all bands of the Ishak. He said this danger would have worst consequences than our kulca's war with the three tribes of cowards. This danger is the white men pouring into our lands. He said we must band together to repel them or we will not survive."

"I did not take much notice of his words at that time, for I did not understand the threat as I do now. My sons are gone above because they were in the company of this white man. I ask that I be permitted to open his body and hang him at the eastern boundary of our land as a warning to any other white men that approach our home."

From the buzz of conversation that ensued following Choc's speech, Nernentou quickly discerned that at least three other warriors agreed with what Choc said and proposed. The remaining five all seemed to await Chaoui's position on the matter.

Chaoui rose and spoke when the murmurs ceased.

"I cannot speak on whether or not the coming of the white men to our lands is a danger to us or not. I know little of the Cannouche except that they do not easily adapt to our way of life and that they smell of drying animal hides."

This elicited chuckles from some of the warriors that was silenced by a wave of Nementou's hand.

"All I can speak of is this particular white man whose fate we are here to decide. This white man is not a warrior of our band, and yet we sit here judging him as if he were. He did not accompany the sons of Choc because he intended to dispose of them but because he was told to accompany them. He is a simple slave that did not do what any of us would have done.

If there is anyone at fault in this matter, it is I; for not teaching him all he should have known of our ways. The white man should not be punished. You may all decide for yourselves whether or not I should be punished."

A chorus of confused mutterings erupted in the hut as Chaoui seated himself. Nementou called twice for silence before order returned to the hut.

"Does anyone else wish to speak?" the chief asked.

There was silence in the hut and Nementou announced that he would speak to Choc and then Chaoui individually at the ceremonial pole and then render his decision.

Fortier and Kata sat anxiously at their unused cook fire as Nementou emerged from the council hut followed by an agitated Choc. Kata strained to hear Choc's words as he and Nementou reached the ceremonial pole, but she was unable to because of the distance. It was obvious though that Choc was angry. After a brief, highly animated monologue by the furious warrior, he turned and stomped back to the council hut. His glance at Fortier turned the Frenchman's blood cold.

Chaoui emerged from the hut and walked slowly to his brother. As he approached the ceremonial pole, he felt Nementou's concentrated appraisal.

"I fear for our village," Nementou began softly. "If I rule in favor of the white man, I believe Choc and his supporters may leave us. We are too few to survive a split. It could be the end of the Vermilion Band."

"I know you will do what you feel you must," Chaoui said. "But I cannot let Choc kill Hiyen. I will do what I must to prevent that from happening."

Chaoui clasped his brother's shoulder affectionately, turned and started for the council hut.

"Chaoui," Nementou whispered after him, "What is it about this white man?"

Chaoui waited a long moment before he answered his brother. He glanced to his hut and saw the faces of Kata and Hiyen staring anxiously at him.

"I did not ask you the reason you brought the white man to the village, and you must not ask me the reason I must save him. I do not think either of us would like hearing our own answers."

Fortier and Kata watched Chaoui return to the council hut after his quiet conversation with Nementou. The chief stood holding the ceremonial pole as if in prayer.

"How long will it take him to make his decision?" Fortier whispered to Kata.

"Until the spirits speak to him."

Soco walked from behind the village midden and joined Kata and Fortier before the hut. As she seated herself next to Kata, the girl spoke softly.

"Pray, Mother, that Chaoui has said the right words that will save Hiyen."

When the old woman did not answer, Kata spoke again, staring intensely at her mother.

"Have I done the right thing by asking Chaoui to save Hiyen, Mother?"

"I do not know, Kata. Only the spirits know if we have done the right thing."

Fortier felt his anxiety taking control. As he sat watching Nementou pray at the red pole, he strongly considered bolting into the forest. He felt sure that Kata and Soco would not raise the alarm, and although his chance of escape was minimal, his chances here in the village seemed dismal. He knew Kata had pleaded with Chaoui to defend him at the council, but he had no idea what Chaoui would actually do.

A light evening breeze wafted through the campsite, stirring the heavy moss draped throughout the surrounding trees. The breeze seemed to whisper the name of Nementou when Fortier saw an ancient warrior in ceremonial garb step from behind the village midden, gleaming ghostly white in the moonlight.

The Frenchman felt a shiver as a wide-eyed Nementou walked slowly to the figure that seemed an apparition. Fortier glanced to his side and saw Kata staring as if in awe at the scene before them. Soco, with a weary look about her, looked only at the ceremonial pole.

Nementou had not been with the spectral figure long when Fortier saw the ancient warrior move into the forest. Nementou turned and strode purposely toward the council hut. All previous indecision seemed gone from the chief as he entered the hut with conviction.

"What in God's name was that?" Fortier whispered.

Kata shook her head and exchanged a few words with her mother. When she turned back to Fortier, her features were distorted with fright.

"She says it was a spirit."

Nementou walked to the front of the assembled warriors and spoke without hesitation.

"Our Grandfathers have spoken to me and decreed that the white man shall not be killed. He is innocent of guilt in the death of the children. Their loss was an act of the gods, and the white man was of no consequence."

Choc erupted from his seated position and rushed to where Nementou stood. For an instant, Nementou thought he would have to defend himself, but Choc whirled to face the warriors and spoke.

"If the white man is not to die, he must at least be banished from the village. He is not one of us, and after this, I am sure no one will allow him in their hut."

Chaoui knew that banishment of Hiyen was no different than a death sentence. He would stand little chance of survival with his limited knowledge of the neighboring tribes and the inherent dangers of the wilderness. Chaoui had not expected the decision Nementou had just announced, and he knew Kata would be elated; but the danger to Hiyen was not past. He stood and spoke loudly.

"A 'life brother' may be banished from the village only for cowardice in battle."

Surprised murmurs and exclamations filled the hut at these words from Chaoui. Nementou waved for order as Choc stammered bitter words.

"Life brother" status is only awarded to someone that gives the gift of life. With this white man, the opposite seems true."

"My woman and I," Chaoui announced, "will soon depart for the lake of sacrifice to pray for a child. Hiyen will accompany us as our protector. He will be aiding the spirits in giving us a child. He will become my 'life brother' when the child is born."

Nementou and the rest of the council hut looked to Choc for further argument. When it was plain that Choc was at a loss for words, Nementou called the end of the council.

After the warriors had noisily filed from the hut, Nementou and Chaoui stood alone with their thoughts. After a moment, they walked together from the hut.

"Do not return too quickly from your journey," Nementou said quietly to Chaoui as they walked to their huts. "Give Choc and his supporters time to forget."

Chaoui nodded and released a strong sigh of exhaustion. He was tired and decided he would not ask Nementou about his decision. His brother would tell him why he had decided to spare Hiyen when he was ready.

As the brothers split for their separate huts, Choc and his woman sat at their cookfire staring intensely at them.

"Chaoui was too clever for you," Choc's woman whispered.

"We will see," Choc spat, "how clever he is with Lacassine,"

For two days the trio had moved in almost absolute silence. Since their departure, Chaoui and Kata had been in a solemn frame of mind. Whenever Fortier attempted to engage Kata in conversation, he received a withering stare from Chaoui that would immediately silence him.

They had followed the bayou that the village was located on far north into Opelousa hunting grounds and for an entire day had moved through pine forests to the river where they were now camped.

When dawn of this third day broke, Fortier walked to the edge of the riverbank. He could see its brownish red banks stretching far into the distance. Chaoui approached from behind and looked north across the river into dense forest.

Pointing west, Fortier spoke with difficulty in Chaoui's language.

"Where river go?"

Chaoui said something that Fortier did not understand so the Frenchman tried again.

"What out there?"

"Caddos," Chaoui answered.

"Are we near the lake?" Fortier asked in French, as Kata joined them.

"The Cata-Oula is not far," the girl answered, "we will reach it today."

"Kata, why did we avoid those little hills we saw yesterday?"

"They are the resting place of an old people. The mounds are old and sacred to all tribes."

So many mysteries, Fortier thought.

It took little time to find a shallow place to cross the river and by mid-day, they had reached their destination. Chaoui chose a bluff near the lake as their encampment. Fortier noticed that the lake was practically surrounded by bluffs.

Near twilight, Chaoui shed his loincloth and weapons and walked to the lake.

"He will return at dawn." Kata said.

"May we speak?" Fortier inquired, "or must you pray also?"

Kata smiled at his ignorance to their customs and told him that they could speak.

They soon finished their meager meal of cured meat slivers and dried corn and as dark descended they gathered pine needles for sleeping pallets. When completed, they lay back listening to the forest sounds and the occasional low chants of Chaoui.

"This Frenchman that taught you my language," Fortier said, "tell me more of him."

"It was long ago," Kata began. "I remember that Soco adopted him, for my father was dead and Soco was the only woman without a man. The men of the village treated him badly at first, for at that time, none of us had seen white men; but he was strong and he stood their abuse."

In the fading light Fortier could just detect a whimsical look come about the girl's face as she continued.

"Every night he would sit in our hut and teach his words to me. He learned to speak in the language of the Ishak, and yet he would only speak to me in his own language, and only listen to me when I spoke to him in Cannouche. He would say that I was the tie to his other world."

"You say he was captured. Where did he come from?"

"He said that he had come from the great water. He had been on a great boat that held many men, and the boat had left he and three others ashore. The four of them had wandered for a long time and his three companions had died. He ate his dog to stay alive for he had no food, and then our warriors found him."

"Did he do women's work as I do?" Fortier asked.

"At first he did, but then after he had been with us for a while, a war party of Kiowa attacked our village. He fought as bravely as any of our warriors and after that he was considered one of us."

"What happened to him, Kata?"

Sadness seemed to ooze from the girl's voice as she continued.

"Some Caddos that we often traded with told the white chief at the post of Natchitoches about the Cannouche that lived with us. One day a group of warriors from the northern post came and offered him a way back to his other world and he went with them."

Fortier settled back against his pallet and gazed up through the scented trees at the dark sky.

"What was the Frenchman's name?"

"Soco called him Cako, for he had much hair on his body as a bear. He called himself Simarre."

The two lay in silence for a while and then Kata murmured softly to the Frenchman.

"The post of Natchitoches is two days walk to the west. If you follow the river of red clay that we crossed you will find the place of your people. When Chaoui completes the sacrifice, you may go to them if you wish."

Fortier took a long time to answer the girl. When he spoke it was in the firm voice of decision.

"I will return to the village, if Chaoui allows that"

"Chaoui would like that," Kata answered smiling.

As the creatures of the forest began to settle down for sleep, Fortier sat staring at the sky. Kata, looking at the dim silhouette of Chaoui, would occasionally turn and look at Fortier's shadow, and then back at Chaoui. Eventually she drifted into a confused sleep.

Fortier kept his watch, knowing that he would return to the village because of his love for this Indian girl. He would pass the road back to civilization, and his only regret was that he respected Chaoui far too much to tell Kata of his love for her.

Fortier awoke from his brief sleep to the sound of Chaoui and Kate conversing. It was the third day and Kata was anxious to return to the village. How Chaoui could sit on a hill and pray all night and then start a long journey was beyond Fortier's comprehension.

The three days had been pleasant for the Frenchman. He had enjoyed Kata's wide-eyed fascination at his stories of the white world. He found it strange that he could not once remember missing that world, even as he spoke of it. Chaoui would sleep much of the morning and then awaken and listen to the stories with Kata translating.

When they started south, Fortier marveled at the brisk pace Chaoui set, considering his all night vigil. When afternoon came and they crossed the river of red clay, Chaoui and Kata moved to a clump of grass and sat to rest.

Fortier knew that they were giving him the opportunity to reconsider his decision. He looked west and knew that his chances of reaching the post were very good. He knew that he should go back to his own kind, for he could never be Ishak.

Kata could never be his woman for she worshipped Chaoui. Fortier knew that the attention she gave to he himself was no more that she would afford a lost puppy. Chaoui and Kata's kindness was probably the result of pity. Why else would Chaoui stand up for him in this matter with the children?

And yet, they had put their trust in him on this journey, even after the disgrace and shame he knew they felt from the loss of the children in the storm. He knew he had been powerless to help those children, but he also knew that the villagers did not believe that. Chaoui and Kata had stood for him through that council of decision, and yet they asked nothing in return from him. For the first time in his life he felt love and the binding relationship of a family that he had never had, in the midst of these primitive people.

"Are you rested enough?" Fortier called to the couple.

Kata spoke to Chaoui and he rose from where he was seated. He walked to where Fortier stood and faced him. Chaoui nodded toward the west with an inquisitive look. Fortier shook his head and pointed toward the south. Chaoui shrugged and struggled with a word and finally said, "Allez."

The three of them turned south laughing.

# CHAPTER 5

The return trip through the pine forest was as enjoyable for Fortier as the three days at the lake of sacrifice had been. Kata and Chaoui were not solemn and quiet as they had been on the way to Cata-Oula, and as they walked through the shadowed forest, each would point to objects or animals they encountered and give the Ishak word for them to Fortier. The Frenchman or Kata would then give the French word for that same thing to Chaoui. There was much laughter at mispronounced words and at some of Fortier's emulations of the strange sounds.

A half-day from the village, they entered a swampy area as they moved south along the bayou on which the village was situated. Fortier was momentarily startled when Chaoui stopped them and indicated silence. He pointed ahead to a large hump on the bank and relieved Fortier's apprehension with a smile.

"What is it?" the Frenchman whispered to Kata

"Alligator, he is enjoying the sun."

"He is huge," Fortier exclaimed quietly. "We should move away from the bayou."

"No Hiyen, he is a gift from the spirits. This is surely a sign that our journey to Cata-Oula has been favorable to them. We will slay him and the village will feast this night."

Chaoui placed his bow and quiver on the ground and moved into the trees. Fortier could see him cutting a sapling from a stout, young oak tree with quick strokes. He then sharpened one end of the branch into a crude spear and began moving toward the monster on the bank without a sound.

'What should I do?" Fortier whispered to Kata.

The girl signed that he should remain quiet.

Chaoui approached the large reptile from its rear end, and coming alongside of it, raised the spear high over his head. He brought the point of the shaft down into the right eye of the sleeping giant and stepped away from its violent thrashing.

"That was well done; and what a large creature. He is longer than I am," Fortier said as he and Kata joined Chaoui.

The Frenchman felt quite helpless but fascinated as he watched the two Ishak work. Chaoui turned the alligator onto its back and cut the body open, down the stomach where the skin seemed thin. He then turned his prize onto its stomach and began cutting long trenches along each side of the backbone. As he would cut, Kata would pull long strips of meat away.

Chaoui then turned the reptile again and removed the internal organs. This completed; he tied the underskin back into place with lengths of vine.

Fortier blanched when Kata, without apparent embarrassment, removed her deerskin skirt and wrapped the meat strips. He could not bring himself to look at her when he spoke.

"Now what do we do?"

"What is wrong, Hiyen?" Kata asked. "Why do you speak to us and yet look away?"

The Frenchman had often heard Kata remove her garments in the hut at night, but had always turned his head away for fear of angering Chaoui.

"I do not wish to embarrass you, Kata."

"I do not know this word, Hiyen," a puzzled Kata answered.

The Frenchman glanced at Chaoui and saw that he was busy making the alligator ready for carrying. He smiled to himself as he thought of the women he had known in his life, for to them, practicality could have never overruled modesty.

"Nevermind, what do we do now?" Fortier said, turning and looking fully at the girl.

"We will carry the carcass back to the village where we will place it into a pit of hot oyster shells. We will cover it with coals and later tonight, the skin will be scorched and the flesh baked. The oil will have gathered in these trenches Chaoui has cut, and we will have a very nice feast."

Fortier's discomfort was rapidly diminishing. The girl was frail and beautiful, void of the heavy deerskin, and he was careful not to let his discomfort become obvious interest.

Early that afternoon they reached the village. Although Chaoui seemed not the least bit hampered by his portion of the heavy load, Fortier was exhausted. When the trio entered the encampment they were met with grim stares. Fortier expected to face this for quite some time, but from the reaction of Kata and Chaoui, it quickly became evident that something was wrong.

Kata stood confused, but after a few glances around the camp, Chaoui knew what was amiss. Whenever he returned to the village from a hunt or raid, the old woman had always been at Kata's side to welcome him.

Nementou approached, and with a melancholy voice, spoke to the travelers.

"Soco has gone to the place above."

Kata lowered her head and Chaoui stared silently at the old woman's meat drying rack.

"When?" Chaoui asked.

"This morning. Her spirit left her body during her sleep."

"Where is her body?"

"We have put her in the sandy ground near the fallen oak."

The travelers walked to the burial spot and stood looking at the shallow grave of the old woman.

"Is this grave satisfactory for so noble a woman?" Fortier asked after a while.

"Her body will not be here long," Kata said sadly. "When the flesh has gone, her bones will be given to a shaman."

As the trio walked back to the camp, Fortier noticed Nementou's woman, Patassa, supervising the cooking of the alligator. He knew that this was one feast they would not be able to enjoy.

Later in the evening, Nementou came to Chaoui's hut. He sat with his brother in silence for a while as Kata prepared moss wicks for the lamps that the alligator oil would afford. Fortier sat beside the oyster shell fireplace looking for large shells suitable for lamps.

Chaoui related to his brother the events of the trip to Cata-Oula. This was followed by a long period of restless silence during which Nementou shifted uncomfortably on the floor of the hut.

"Are you troubled, my brother?" Chaoui asked when the silence in the hut became awkward.

Nementou leaned in close to Chaoui and spoke in a secretive manner.

"The powerful shaman, Lacassine visited us two nights ago. He has learned of the white man, Chaoui. He wants me to give Hiyen to him."

Kata stopped her work and listened intently. Fortier felt the sudden tension in the hut and strained to understand as many words as he could.

"I am ashamed, for I was afraid to refuse Lacassine and insult him, for I have heard that his power and influence is great. But before I could speak a word, Soco intervened and said that the white man was hers. She actually stood before Lacassine and told him that the white man was hers and that he could not have him."

Chaoui and Kata exchanged smiles at this news; they would have expected no less from the old woman.

"Choc has spoken in favor of Lacassine and the people are listening to him," Nementou continued. "He says that Soco's insult to Lacassine brought about her death, and that I should give Hiyen to Lacassine to protect the village from his magic."

Kata started to intercede but was silenced by a look from Chaoui.

"And what do you think you should do, brother?" Chaoui asked quietly.

Nernentou shifted again in indecision and his eyes never left the ground when he spoke.

"Our village seems cursed as long as this white man is among us. First the episode at the great water, now this. Chaoui, our kulca started the Vermilion Band; I cannot let endearment to a captive endanger the village."

Fortier whispered urgently to Kata to please interpret the conversation taking place. Chaoui harshly signed to him to remain silent.

"What do you think you should do, Nementou?" Chaoui repeated.

"He is not one of us. I think I should listen to the people."

"Please Nementou," Kata cried, "Lacassine will surely kill him."

"Silence!" Chaoui exclaimed, staring into Kata's eyes.

"If I am to remain Chief of the Vermilion Band I must listen to the will of its people. When Lacassine returns, I will give the white man to him."

Nementou rose and left the hut. Kata lowered her head and stared at the moss between her fingers.

"Kata, what is wrong?" Fortier pleaded. "I know this concerns me."

The girl looked at the Frenchman with sadness and whispered,

"Hiyen, you should have gone to your people. I should have forced you to go to your people."

"What has happened?" Fortier asked again with panic in his voice.

"Lacassine is a powerful shaman of a neighboring village. He hates the white men for he says that they will drive us from this land just as the Caddos drove us from our homes in the north long ago. He believes that white men that come here must die. Soco tried to prevent him from taking you and now she is dead. Nementou says he must give you to Lacassine."

Fortier rose, glancing around quickly as a trapped animal.

"Wait," Kata said. "Lacassine is not here yet. You must leave tonight when the village is asleep and find your way to the river of red clay. Follow it west to the French post; you will find safety there."

"Kata, what do you tell him?" Chaoui asked quietly.

The girl looked deep into Chaoui's eyes and knew that she could not lie to him.

"I am telling him to flee for his life."

Chaoui looked long at his woman. He still could not quite identify what Kata was feeling for this white man, and it troubled him, for he had understood everything about her prior to Hiyen's presence. The pleading look that she gave him melted his indecision. He felt his love for her swell within him and once again, he committed himself.

"Kata, do you think I would give my 'life-brother' to that devil?"

Tears welled in Kata's eyes and she slumped with relief. She turned to Fortier and smiled to try to relieve some of the tension she felt radiating from him.

"If we help Hiyen," the girl said, "we may not be safe from Lacassine ourselves."

Looking directly at Fortier and speaking in a decisive manner, Chaoui addressed his woman.

"Our white brother has learned much about our world here, and now you and I shall learn about his at the white post."

Kata gazed at Chaoui in amazement. A flurry of excited thoughts scurried through her mind and yet she could not speak any of them.

'Tell Hiyen to sleep now," Chaoui directed. "When the light of the moon has faded, we will leave."

"But Nementou…" Kata began.

"He will forgive us," Chaoui said. "He will have much time to forgive us before he sees us again."

"When will we return, Chaoui?"

Chaoui looked at Fortier and then at Kata and mumbled as if to himself.

"Our destiny is in the hands of the spirits."

Fortier felt a hand shake him and he opened his eyes. It was dark as pitch in the hut but he could tell that Chaoui and Kate were both awake from their movements. He had been reluctant to allow himself sleep because of his fear and yet he was confident that Chaoui and Kata would not betray him. He had feared that the shaman would come while they slept but Chaoui had insisted that they rest. It had been what seemed to Fortier a long time before he had slept.

Fortier felt helpless as he followed Chaoui and Kate out of the hut into the dark encampment.

"What about the dogs?" Fortier whispered, knowing that the spotted village curs were the encampment sentries.

"They will be silent," Kata answered. "They know us."

The trio had gathered few articles in order to move quickly. Moving quietly from the village, as Kata had predicted, the dogs were silent. When the first turn of the bayou was reached, Chaoui stopped and turned to the village. He mumbled a few words and then quickly began walking to the north.

"What did he say, Kata?" Fortier asked.

"He was saying good-bye to the village."

"Fortier ran ahead and grabbed Chaoui's arm, stopping him. Kata moved up to them quietly with a puzzled look.

"What is it, Hiyen?"

"I don't want you to come, neither of you. There is no need for you to accompany me. I can find my own way. Stay here where you both belong."

After a brief exchange between Kata and Chaoui, the girl spoke urgently to the Frenchman.

"Chaoui says that without him, Lacassine will catch you and kill you for having lived among us. Chaoui can show you a faster way to the French post than by way of Cata-Oula. This is your only chance."

Fortier felt affection and shame sweep over him equally. Affection for Chaoui because of his unselfishness, and shame for mentally coveting this brave man's wife.

Impulsively, the Frenchman clasped Chaoui's shoulders and looked into his eyes.

"Kata," Fortier said with emotion, "Your word for brother."

"Hacka," a smiling Kata answered.

Gazing into the wild, yet innocent eyes of the warrior, Fortier recalled the first time he had looked into those eyes; when he had been tied to a tree and Chaoui had squatted before him brandishing a knife.

"Hacka!" Fortier nodded to Chaoui.

Chaoui looked to Kata and shrugged.

"Allez," Chaoui whispered and trotted to the north.

# CHAPTER 6

❀

The trio traveled at a brisk pace, well into the afternoon, into the Opelousa hunting grounds. On the morning of the second day, Fortier noticed that they turned northwest. Had he been alone, he would have continued north as they had done on their trip to Cata-Oula, and lost countless hours of time.

At mid-morning they moved past a small lake and the terrain changed from the flat hardwood forests to thick pine tree covered hill country. Chaoui stopped them suddenly and Fortier became instantly alarmed as the Ishak quickly strung his bow. Kata moved to cover and Chaoui turned and signed that the Frenchman should draw his knife from its sheath.

As Fortier swept the surrounding area with a glance, two scrawny, stoop-shouldered Indians emerged from the trees. One held a club and the other a pitiful bow that seemed almost childlike.

"These are not Opelousa," Kata whispered.

"They are Chatots," Chaoui said, never taking his eyes from the small warriors. "They are few and timid. If they notice Hiyen's white skin they will probably run."

"Greetings to our northern neighbors," Chaoui said in a mixture of Ishak and sign language. "We are crossing your land, bound north. We go to the post of the Cannouche for trade."

As Chaoui spoke, the little men seemed to shrink with apprehension. Timidly, they moved away from the trio.

"Go, do not hunt," one of the Chatots signed.

Chaoui nodded and signaled for Kata to join them. As they moved past the small Indians, one of the Chatots, looking closely at Fortier, released an audible gasp. Chaoui motioned for Fortier and Kata to hurry on and they had taken no more than ten steps when Fortier turned and saw that the little men had vanished.

They moved steadily through the day and camped on a small hill at dark. They made their meager camp hastily to afford as much sleeping time as possible.

"Is there a chance Lacassine can catch us?" Kata asked, removing food from her bundle.

"Lacassine is a powerful shaman," Chaoui said, "No one knows what he can do. If he learns or figures that we have gone to the post of the Cannouche, he may catch us."

"But where else could we have gone?" Fortier asked after Kata's translation.

"To the Karankawas, our neighbors to the west," Kata said. "Or to the great water and east by pirogue."

"Then I should think that we are safe. How can Lacassine cover all three routes?"

"He will have runners cover them," Kata said. "They will find out for him."

"By tracking us?" Fortier queried.

"Yes, by tracking us, or by getting information from anyone that has seen…"

Kata cut her words short and turned quickly to Chaoui.

"The Chatots, they will tell Lacassine of us."

"Yes, they might," Chaoui said with a knowing look. "And that is why I must go back."

"But how can that help?" Kata asked.

There was no answer from Chaoui and immediately fear and concern overcame Kata. There was an edge of panic in her voice when she addressed her husband again.

"What do you intend to do, Chaoui?"

"I intend to do nothing to the Chatots. Listen to me, Kata. We do not know if Lacassine has sent runners. We may be running from nothing but our own fear. Lacassine may have already forgotten about Hiyen once he went to our village and found him gone. That is, if he has even gone to our village yet to claim him. He knew that Nernentou was going to turn Hiyen over to him, so he may not have been in such a rush to come for Hiyen."

"But what if he has sent runners?" Kata asked.

"Then I must stop them from returning to Lacassine."

Kata turned to Fortier and translated the parts of the conversation he had not understood. Fortier signed to Chaoui that he wished to accompany him.

"Tell Hiyen," Chaoui said to Kata, "that I can do what I must do better on my own."

Kata translated for she knew that Chaoui was right. She had heard many of the village warriors say that his prowess in the forest was unequaled. Fortier would only impede his action, if it came to that. Her apprehension lessened when she realized that perhaps Chaoui's theory was correct. Lacassine may have forgotten about Hiyen after his escape. They may indeed be only running from their own fear.

"I should be gone for no more than two days," Chaoui said. "If it takes me more than that, you are to both go on to the white post and I will join you there. Not much farther on, you will meet the river of red clay. Follow it to the west and it will lead to the white men's town."

After Kata had translated the salient points of the conversation Fortier had missed, she busied herself preparing a meal. She was silent and Chaoui approached her from behind and caressed her gently.

"Do not be afraid, Kata."

"But I am afraid," Kata said without turning. "I do not know if I will be accepted at the white post."

Chaoui turned and without a word, sadly crept onto his sleeping pallet of pine needles for a few hours of rest before his mission.

Chaoui set out early the next morning before Kata and Fortier had risen. When Fortier awoke, he saw Kata removing fishing utensils from her bundle. She walked to the little stream near their camp, waded into the water and stood poised. The small darts she held were as long as a man's hand, made of branches with a piece of bone at the end.

Three times she spotted a prey, and throwing, missed her mark. Fortier could not prevent himself from laughing as Kata's temper built. When he had enjoyed a hearty laugh, he called to the girl.

"Kata, come out of there; my bundle is full of smoked fish. I do not think Chaoui took any of it."

"He must have taken some," Kata called from the stream.

"We surely won't starve," Fortier said with authority. "Now come out of there."

The stern manner in which Fortier had spoken made Kata stare for a moment. She emerged from the water looking at him intently.

"Hiyen, it is time you took a woman."

"Why do you say that?" a startled Fortier asked.

"I think you need someone to care for," Soco said shyly.

"I care for you, Kata," Fortier mumbled hoarsely.

Long moments passed and an awkward silence ensued. Fortier thought of all Chaoui had done and was presently doing and broke his own reverie.

"I care for Chaoui also, and I cared for Soco."

For the first time since Fortier had known Kata, she seemed nervous. She flitted around the small campsite for a few moments and then sat before Fortier.

"Let us work for a while on your use of my language," Kata said. She seemed happy to have found some other subject to raise.

"First, tell me more of your people," Fortier said. "I would like to know the background of your people as well as your language."

Kata frowned in puzzlement. "What do you wish to know?" she asked.

"Why are your villages so small and scattered?"

The girl smiled as pleasant memories of evenings near warm oyster shell ovens with blustery winds on the outside of her mother's hut flooded her mind. She began the oratory she had heard Soco recite many times.

"Long ago our people were the most powerful tribe in this land. We had many enemies and every other tribe dreaded us. Most of our war chiefs were hostile to anyone not of our tribe and our only friends were the Chitimachas."

"The Opelousa, Choctaw and Alibamons finally formed an alliance against us. There were a few small battles that had no results; and then our villages joined to try to destroy the alliance. A large number of our warriors went to meet the warriors of what our war chiefs called 'the three tribes of cowards'; only they were not cowards. They met on the little hills southeast of our village in a large battle. Our warriors fought bravely but they were outnumbered. Also, our braves were fighting for more hunting grounds and superiority whereas the alliance was fighting for survival. They were desperate and they almost annihilated our warriors. The survivors fled back to their villages or were taken prisoner and made slaves. The large villages dispersed into small, nomadic groups and have remained that way."

"Our numbers grow smaller and I suppose our people will never be powerful again. At least we have become, as you say, more civilized as a people. We have left off from quite a few terrible practices we once had."

"Such as?" Fortier asked hesitantly.

"Hostile rituals that you would not understand," Kata said quietly.

Fortier shuddered, thinking of the rumors he had heard in New Orleans about the mysterious Atakapa. He decided to remain silent when he noticed that Kata had sunk into a deep melancholy.

"One of the principal chiefs at the battle of the little hills was Chaoui and Nementou's Kulca," Kata said after a brief silence.

"Their Kulca?" Fortier asked.

"Yes, their father's father," Kata explained. "He was called Chataign and he was very brave and respected. He was killed there and Chaoui and Nementou never knew him, but their father spoke of him always."

"If Chaoui is like him," Fortier said, "I'm sure he was a great man."

"Chaoui is good," Kata said with a smile. "And you are good too, Hiyen."

"I have learned much about good since I have been with the Vermilion Band," Fortier said. "I will never be happy until I earn a new name from you, though," the Frenchman continued with a smile.

"Perhaps you must make that name for yourself, Hiyen. You must call yourself what you feel you should be known as."

Fortier did not answer and sat musing over the advice.

"Now," Kata said, "on with your language lesson."

Chaoui passed the place they had seen the Chatots and continued his brisk pace. He knew that his chances of finding the two small warriors were slim and they were of no concern to him. He must concentrate on intercepting Lacassine's runner. He hoped to surprise and capture the runner, but if necessary, he was prepared to kill him. He would do anything to insure the safety of Kata.

The story he had fabricated for Kata about the possibility that Lacassine may have forgotten about Hiyen had been the first untruth he had ever told Kata. He could not recall ever telling an untruth to anyone, but in this case he had felt it necessary to do so.

Chaoui had decided that Kata should have the opportunity to find out if life at the white man's post was what she wanted, and she should have that opportunity without his presence. He would afford her a few days there alone. When he joined her, if she seemed content, he would make his own decision as to whether he could stay there or not. If she did not seem content, they would move westward. He had always wished to see the great hill far to the west that had saved his people during the great flood, before the time of his Kulca's Kulca. He would miss Nementou sorely, but he would accept their fate, whatever it may be.

Chaoui worked his way through a large deadfall of pine into a clearing scanning the ground before him. He froze when he saw the prints. A few moments of scrutiny told him unwelcome news. His years of reading the signs of the forest floor told him that the two Chatots had met a group of men here. The two small warriors had departed to the east. The group of prints that headed to the northwest was Ishak moccasins. Five of them and moving quickly. Could the devil Laccasine be among them? It would not surprise Chaoui for the shaman's magic was strong.

Chaoui sat to decide on a plan of action for he knew that haste and panic would not serve him well in this situation. He knew that the trackers chances of catching up to Kata and Hiyen were good. Kata would be killed and Hiyen taken back to Lacassine's village for ceremony. If he himself overtook this party of warriors, what would he do? Could he actually stalk and kill five Ishak because of Kata's fancy? He knew Kata was very fond of Hiyen because he reminded her of the Frenchman from her childhood. Had her feelings gone beyond fondness?

Kata would be a stranger at the white post just as Hiyen was with the Ishak. Hiyen had tried hard to adopt their ways, but he was still strange to them. Would the same hold true for Kata? Would she always be strange to the whites?

It also greatly troubled Chaoui to know that Lacassine was probably right. The white men would eventually bring about the end of their way of life. The harsh tasting water and sickness that they had already given to some of the tribes on the great river was making their numbers short. Of course, Lacassine's notion of killing all white men was absurd; they were far too many and it was not right. He was sure that his father would not have approved of Lacassine's method. He must follow his instincts and protect Kata. He came out of his reverie and rose to set out at all haste to overtake the party of Ishak. He looked to the world above and prayed that he would not be too late. He took two steps and gasped when he saw Lacassine and four warriors step from behind trees into the clearing.

# CHAPTER 7

*F*ortier and Kata were irritable and worried. It was the morning of the third day since Chaoui's departure and they were both experiencing unfavorable premonitions. For long periods each would stare expectantly in the direction Chaoui had left two days before. The time had come to continue their journey, as Chaoui had instructed, but neither wished to voice this fact.

"I find it strange that we have not encountered any hunting parties from the post," Fortier said, trying to make conversation.

Kata broke her concentrated staring to the southeast and smiled to the Frenchman absentmindedly. Fortier marveled at the girl's courage and he felt a wave of affection for her sweep over him. He rose from his squat and gathered his pack to him.

"Come Kata, it is time to be off."

A quick, pained expression flitted across Kata's face, but she quickly composed her features. Kata was inwardly cursing herself for having been so selfish. How could she have thought only of visiting the white post and not been more cognizant of the danger Chaoui was going off to face? She was sure now that Chaoui had belittled the threat he was facing so that she would not worry about him or try to stop him. After two days of waiting, she was sure that things could not have gone well or Chaoui would be back by now.

The pair gathered their scant belongings. Fortier in a hasty manner, and the girl slowly, as if in a trance.

"I will lead," Fortier said. "Let us move quickly but without any sound. We will pretend we are again on our way to Cata-Oula."

His attempt to cheer Kata was futile for her expression remained downcast. Her expression changed to puzzlement when she saw Fortier strike out to the southeast.

"Hiyen, we must do as Chaoui said," she said, realizing what he intended.

"If some ill has befallen Chaoui, he may need my help," Fortier said sternly, "Chaoui has done much for me and perhaps now I may be able to repay a little of his unselfishness,"

"I have never disobeyed Chaoui," the girl pleaded.

"Chaoui may need our help," Fortier exclaimed. "Please do not make excuses about obedience to Chaoui when truly you merely lack confidence in my abilities."

Fortier said these words with such emotion that he surprised himself. As Kata stood staring at him, he sighed and slumped into a crouch.

"Even I lack confidence in my abilities," he whispered. "It has always been so easy to run away, Kata. I have never been able to understand that part of myself. A profound uncaring about anyone and everything but myself has always been my way. Since I have been here, I fancied that I had changed; that I could actually experience friendship and love; emotions that have always eluded me."

"I had actually found myself liking this new Gabriel Fortier or Hiyen or whatever I may be called. At least before the children were lost in the storm. And now, just because the path back to my old lifestyle is right before me, I will not allow myself to take it so easily. Perhaps now I can really atone for the loss of the children, in your eyes and Chaoui's, as well as my own. If this is some sort of spiritual test your spirits or my God is giving me, I'm going to succeed at it."

Kata shook her head and spoke with evident fear in her voice.

"I understand little of what you have said, Hiyen; but if you mean that it will be harmful for you to return to your people; don't you realize what returning to my people means?"

"Yes, it means leaving a place I want to remain in because of one man."

"Lacassine is more than a man," Kata retorted, "He is a powerful shaman and all of our people respect him."

"What you mean," Fortier said gesturing heavily, "is that all of your people fear him. He will not stop the white man, Kata. He may kill me or a hundred like me, but he will not stop us. He should welcome those like me that wish to live in your manner, with you."

"And what of those," Kata said thoughtfully, "that do not wish to live in our manner? The gossip says that Lacassine preaches that the white men will drive us from this land."

Fortier stepped back in embarrassment and turned away from the girl.

"Forgive me, Kata, I have been presumptuous. We will go and find Chaoui and then I will return to my people."

"Oh Hiyen," Kata said angrily, "Can't you understand? I do not want you to go. You are…Oh, I cannot explain what I feel. I am afraid of what I feel."

Fortier looked at the girl lovingly and voiced his thoughts.

"My poor little Kata, I have caused one so innocent to experience divided loyalties."

'Please explain…"

"It doesn't matter," Fortier interrupted. "I suppose you have done the same thing to your Chaoui. Lacassine may be partially correct; even white men with no ill intentions are harmful to your people. Come, we will find Chaoui and then I will return to my people."

"Hiyen, please!" Kata pleaded.

Fortier walked to the girl and cupped her face in his hands. "Do not worry, Kata," he whispered. "I will depart as your friend. I will never forget you or Chaoui because of the better man you have made me into. You and Chaoui will return to your village. I am sure Nementou will protect you."

Fortier had decided to turn himself over to the shaman. He did not fancy himself the sacrificial type, but he was pleased to know that he would do it willingly to protect the only loved ones he had ever known. Strange, he thought, are all men finally content with themselves whey they find something they are willing to die for? He took Kata's hand, started walking to the southeast, and muttered in the broken English he had learned on the river.

"The only thing I will miss is an Indian girl dressed in tree moss."

"I do not understand your words," Kata said.

"I said, let us go and find my friend, your man."


Chaoui froze in place. He knew that any hasty action would cause violence and death. He decided to remain silent until one of the five before him spoke.

"You have been thinking a long time," Lacassine said, advancing. "Have you misplaced something?"

Chaoui had trouble meeting the steely eyes of the shaman.

"I will not play word games with you, Lacassine. My woman and the white man have reached the white post by now; they are safe from you."

"Your woman never had anything to fear from me," the shaman said. "I only wished to rid our land of another cursed white man."

"Why?" Chaoui exclaimed. "What harm would one white man have been to our people?"

"I am looking at the harm he has done." Lacassine said. "This harmless white man has come and gone and he has taken one of us with him and infected your soul. He has made you wish to see his villages and forget that you are Ishak and belong here. As more of them come here, we will suffer all the more. They will eradicate us, we will vanish from this land and no one will even know of our people or what became of us. I will go to any measure to stop them."

"This white man is my friend," Chaoui exclaimed. "He did not ask for me to adopt his ways, he tried to adopt mine."

"He wished to know us to destroy us," the shaman blurted.

"That is not what I believe," Chaoui stated.

One of the warriors in Lacassine's party stepped up beside the shaman and only then did Chaoui recognize Choc, from his own village. Chaoui flushed, realizing he had been that preoccupied with the shaman.

"You fool," Choc spat out the words. "Do you defend this white man for what he means to you or what he means to your woman?"

"Do not risk losing your tongue, Choc," Chaoui said quietly.

"And have you lost your eyes?" Choc continued. "This white man and your woman are together much more than you realize. None of us know what their words are to each other, not even you. Everyone knows that the white man wants Kata for his woman."

"Choc, you are a liar and my enemy," Chaoui said, drawing his knife.

Lacassine restrained Choc as he also went for his weapon.

"Chaoui," the shaman said, "If Choc lies, why have the white man and your woman gone on without you?"

Chaoui relaxed his fighting crouch and stared at Choc for a moment before he answered. His mind raced for words that the shaman would believe.

"My woman is to wait for me at the white post. I was returning to make my peace with you so that we nay return to our village without fear of reprisal."

"Very well," Lacassine said, "You have made your peace with me. Now come, we will return to our villages."

"I must go and get my woman," Chaoui said.

"Forget the woman," Lacassine retorted. "From what Choc has said, she will be better off with the Cannouche. You may get another woman that is not so fond of white men."

"I will return to my village after I have gone for my woman," Chaoui insisted.

"Chaoui," Lacassine said impatiently, "I cannot allow you to go to the white post. Once there, you will not return. The woman is nothing, but I need every warrior."

"I am not your warrior," Chaoui shouted.

"Then you are my enemy!" Lacassine screamed.

Just as the shaman's scream rang out, Choc hurtled himself at Chaoui. The knife Chaoui had drawn had never been replaced and the upturned blade caught the warrior low in the stomach. Chaoui felt the hot blood gush over his hand and he tumbled to free himself from the grunting form of Choc. As he lunged back to his feet, an arrow pierced his left shoulder. The warrior that had loosed this arrow advanced with a war club and Chaoui threw his knife. The warrior turned and the weapon sunk into his side. As he fell to the ground screaming, Chaoui ran to gain cover to string his bow.

The other two warriors that accompanied Lacassine had been rendered helpless by the presence of the shaman himself, for although they stood with bows drawn, the shaman had been standing between them and Chaoui. When Chaoui dashed for cover, they both loosed their arrows. One missile flew close over the weaving Chaoui's head and the other thunked solidly into his left rear thigh. He fell heavily against a clump of brush and tried frantically to string his bow.

He was dimly aware of the two warriors taking aim while the shaman stood to the side regarding him with hate-filled eyes. He tasted the salt of his own tears as he realized that he would never see his beloved Kata again. It did not matter if she loved Hiyen. He was a good man and now that he was dying, Hiyen would care for her in his white world. But Lacassine must be stopped.

He saw through his blurred vision the bowstring slip onto the notch just as two arrows thudded into his chest. His scream rang through the clearing.

'Kataaaa…"

The two bowmen approached Lacassine, shaking their heads. Lacassine's rage subsided a bit and he surveyed the area with a look of disgust.

"Both dead," the shaman hissed, "and Chaoui too. I should not have let this happen. Ishak should only die killing white men."

"What form of spell could the white man have cast for Chaoui to die for him?" one of the warriors asked.

"The white men," Lacassine said, "are powerful in many ways besides their numbers."

"Shall we pursue?" asked the warrior.

The shaman looked to the northwest and then spoke quietly.

"No, if they have not reached the white post, they are too near for us to endanger ourselves in pursuit. We will return to our people. This white man is gone, but many more will be coming and I have much to do in preparation for them."

Fortier was well aware of the fact that he was not a competent tracker. Kata had left the pursuit of Chaoui to him so he was completely elated when they found the place in which they had encountered the Chatots. Kata sensed his relief and told him that he was learning much more than just the Ishak language. He acknowledged the compliment with an embarrassed chuckle.

They decided to stop for the night and continue their trek at first light. Neither offered conversation as they lay on opposite sides of a fallen log. Fortier kept his ears attentive to the sounds of the forest as he prepared to let Kata sleep for a few hours, after which he would then awaken her for her turn at standing watch.

He soon heard the steady sound of her breathing and knew that she was asleep. He wrapped his arms around himself as the first chill of the season touched him. He thought of how winter was indeed coming quickly to this marshy land he had come to love. Soon the rains would begin, with the temperature failing occasionally to near freezing. At those times, the high humidity would indeed make for cold winter nights.

Suddenly he thought of the Opelousa. He had known little about this man. If not for some whim of Nementou, he and the Opelousa would be laying trap lines now. A mild winter and a little luck would have taken him back to New Orleans a wealthy man; wealthy at least by his standards. There would have been plenty of money for…and that is as far as his planning had taken him. Plenty of money for what? A month? Six months? Whatever the time it would have afforded him, it would not have concluded anything. Eventually he would have gone searching again. Searching for happiness, for security, for meaning. Searching for Gabriel Fortier.

Instead, here he was, lying next to the answer. He sat up and looked over the log at the girl lying in deep sleep. The crude deerskin skirt did little to accentuate the brown smoothness of her legs. The callused, work-stained hands were anything but delicate. The flat and square cut of her black hair would have been scoffed at by any French lady. But she was beauty to Fortier. She, this land and the existence offered simplicity that Fortier wanted to be a part of. And, since he could not, he would at least ensure that she remained a part of it.

His thoughts roamed over a variety of subjects until he felt that half of the darkness had passed. He touched Kata and she came awake with a start. When he was sure that she was completely awake, he allowed himself to drift off to sleep, dreaming of tranquil forests and an Ishak maiden.

A shaft of sunlight and the tapping of a woodpecker on a nearby tree woke Fortier. The rich smell of a magnolia haunted his nose and brought him to reality. He sat up and saw that Kata was gone. He started to call out but decided to look about for her instead. Momentarily, he saw her some distance away, standing at the edge of what appeared to be a clearing,

"Why didn't you wake me?" Fortier asked as he approached the girl.

His words caught short when he noticed what held her gaze. Lying on the ground, twenty meters away, was a small deerskin pouch with a colorful strap. He knew instantly that it was Chaoui's pouch. Turning to the girl, he saw she stared with an unblinking expression.

At the same instant, they both noticed a section of beaten down grass. As Kata began to advance toward it, Fortier caught her arm.

"Wait here, I will go and see."

She looked at him strangely and walked past. They advanced slowly upon the spot to find three fresh piles of moist dirt. Kata released a hollow, mournful moan that wrenched Fortier's heart. When the Frenchman spoke, his voice had a high pitch that quivered with emotion.

"He may have…We do not know…"

He cut his thoughtless stammer short when Kata ran to a nearby tree and began breaking off a stout limb. Fortier ran to her and attempted to restrain her.

"Kata…you cannot do this."

He was startled by the contorted look on her face. Her eyes were glossy and her features were pulled taut. She seemed inordinately strong. With all of his strength, the Frenchman pulled her away from the tree.

"Kata, I will do it."

She ceased her struggle and stepped away. Fortier never took his eyes from her as he fought the limb from the tree. She seemed in a trance as they walked to the fresh mounds of soil. Fortier mumbled a half-forgotten prayer as he began scraping the dirt from the first mound. Kata rocked back and forth on her heels and chanted under her breath, alternating her glance from the sky above them to the hole Fortier was digging.

The Frenchman felt bile rise in his throat when the limb pushed against something soft in the dirt. Kata stopped her chant and stared intently into the shallow grave. Fortier fought the growing nausea as he located the head of the corpse and moved the soil away from it.

Whether from some distinct facial feature, or some other characteristic, Kata knew that it was Chaoui before Fortier cleared the dirt from the waxen face. Her wail pierced the morning and quieted every sound that had thus far brightened the day. She fell to her knees and pounded the earth as if to punish it for what it held. Fortier sat there, trying desperately to rub the sting from his eyes.

The two of them remained that way for most of the morning. Kata, with her face pressed to the ground, and Fortier, slumped over, staring into the grave. When the sun reached its zenith, Fortier moved to the next mound and began scraping dirt. He worked quickly with no perception of his surroundings. He uncovered both cadavers and fell to the ground, breathing heavily. He recovered his strength after a while and then quickly re-covered the dead. Turning from the grisly task, he noticed Kata was gone.

Walking away from the graves, he began to trot for the camp when he remembered that Kata had a fishknife. He could not let her do anything foolish. He came upon Kata, sitting on the log they had slept beside, as if waiting for him. He gasped when he saw her, for she had indeed used the fishknife. She had cut all of the hair from her head and sat chanting unintelligibly. She did not return his eye contact when he squatted before her.

"One was Choc, from the village," Fortier said. "The other I have never seen; he did not wear the trappings of a shaman."

Kata rose from the log and picked up her belongings.

"I will kill Lacassine for this," Fortier continued, "Somehow, I will kill him."

Kata did not look at the Frenchman when she spoke. Her voice was a sorrowful whisper.

"Go back to your people, Hiyen."

"Kata, no!" Fortier pleaded, advancing to her.

"I cannot look upon you," the girl cried. "We share the guilt of Chaoui's death. Now we must both go back to our people and live with it."

"I will not let Chaoui go unavenged," Fortier exclaimed.

"You must," Kate returned. "Lacassine is much more clever than you think. If you attempt to kill him, you will die. I want you to live, for I love you, and for that I deserve to live with this guilt."

Fortier stood staring vacantly at the girl as she began to move away.

"Kata, please."

"Go and live, Hiyen," Kata said sternly, without turning. "I beg this of you. Do not go to Lacassine's village and die and do not ask me to go with you to your people. This would dishonor Chaoui and his death."

Kata ran into the forest without looking back or speaking again. Fortier stood staring until she was out of sight. He walked to the pack she had left and scooped it up. He crushed the pouch between his hands as he felt hot tears well to his eyes. He fought to control the sobs as he began walking to the northwest.

Fortier had no idea how far he had walked when the sun began its fall to the west. He stopped, slumping down against a large pine and cursed himself. What can you do to this Lacassine? he thought, you who sits and whimpers like a babe.

A small gray squirrel moving down the trunk of a nearby tree stopped and looked at him. It's face was the face of the frontier girl that had challenged him with her eyes in St. Louis, and it was smiling.

"Run little Frenchman, run," the squirrel chattered.

Fortier threw a branch and the squirrel scampered back to the heights of the tree.

He realized that he must have slept when he felt a cold, dripping rain bead his face. The morning was gray and overcast and the wet forest chilled him to shivers. He rose and attached the pouch to his waist and began his journey.

Somehow, he would find the village of Lacassine. He would kill the shaman at any cost.

He had been prepared to give his life before to save Chaoui and Kata, and now he would give it if necessary, to avenge Chaoui. Kata need never know of his quest. Let her believe him to be back with his people, it was better this way.

He knew that he would probably die, but he had to find a way to take Lacassine with him. He looked to the heavens as he walked and cried out in a loud voice.

"Great Spirit, I am no longer Gabriel Fortier. I am no longer Hiyen. I am now only 'he who lives to kill Lacassine.'"

# CHAPTER 8

*A*fter two days of travel Fortier began to recognize some of the physical features of the land. His senses were hampered by lack of food and he knew that this was also affecting him physically. It had become more and more difficult to continue walking for lack of strength.

He had grown accustomed to the dull pain in the pit of his stomach, but occasional spasms of nausea began to overcome him. He had little luck trying to assemble snares he had seen the village boys use that had seemed so simple. Given time, he was sure he would have been able to manufacture some form of snaring device, but he wanted to lose as little time as possible. He feared Lacassine's village might move before he could reach it. He knew that this would be no easy task, having never been to the shaman's village, but he was confident he could find it from the information Kata had supplied about surrounding Ishak sites.

When he met the bayou that the Vermilion Band village was situated on, he guessed that he was not more than a few kilometers away from that site. He prayed that no one from Nementou's camp would encounter him for fear that Kata would learn of his return. He turned west and felt anxiety crawl over him as he plunged into wilderness he had never entered.

The dizziness hit him like a blow when it came. For the past two hours it had crept up on him slowly and then dissipated at intervals. This time its force caused him to stagger as he began to chant to himself a rivermans ditty from his keelboat days. He stumbled on blindly and realized with a start that he was chanting the old song of the river in Ishak. This seemed insanely funny to the Frenchman and he began to laugh as he fell to his knees.

His laugh was cut short when he looked up and saw the warrior standing before him. The facial features of the Indian were blurred, but Fortier knew that it had to be Lacassine. He mustered his strength and stood.

"I will kill you, Lacassine," he muttered.

Fortier took two steps toward the brave and fell to the ground unconscious.

When Fortier awoke and looked about he recognized nothing. He lay on flattened grass amidst a group of widely scattered oak trees. As his vision cleared, he saw a small pond of murky water not far from his makeshift bed. The water occasionally bubbled as if something beneath it stirred. The bare ground around the pond gave it an eerie appearance.

Not far away he could see the bayou, if indeed it was the same bayou, not remembering how far he had traveled. He turned and saw the old Indian taking two fat quail from the spit they had roasted on over a small fire. The Frenchman moved to a sitting position and began to speak, but was silenced by the old man.

"Here, eat, talk later," the old man said.

Fortier's astonishment caused him to pause momentarily, then he ripped into the dripping bird. He eyed the old man curiously as he ate. The old Indian's actions were so matter-of-fact that Fortier was puzzled.

When the Frenchman finished the quail he was handed a small portion of dried corn. He muttered a hesitant 'thank you' and continued his much-needed feast.

When only a few kernels of corn remained, the old man spoke.

"You would not have killed Lacassine for you would not have found him."

"How you know...?" Fortier stuttered in his limited Ishak.

"I know," the old man interrupted, "I know of Chaoui's death and I know that Kata is safe."

The ancient warrior pulled a tattered hide around his thin shoulders as a chilly, humid wind tugged at him. He looked gravely into the Frenchman's eyes.

"Do you wish to kill Lacassine because of Chaoui or because you are white?"

Fortier was astonished at the old man's knowledge.

"Chaoui my friend," Fortier said. "Lacassine no kill all whites."

"That is right," the old man answered. "There are many whites in our land now, but there was only one in an Ishak village, and he could not allow that."

Fortier's puzzled look deepened and the old man continued.

"Do you understand my words?"

"Yes...No..." Fortier answered.

"I mean," the old man went on as if speaking to a child, "that Lacassine wants to drive the white men out of this land. He has been visiting many villages of many tribes. He has visited the Chitimacha and the Avoyels. He has sent runners to the Washa, the Chawasha and the Houmas to come and talk of war. If these tribes join him, he may convince the Natchez to participate and there will be much bloodshed."

Fortier sat staring at the old man as if bewildered. Could he be believed? Was this conspiracy of Lacassine genuine or the raving of some ancient lunatic?

The old man seemed to sense Fortier's disbelief and waved it off.

"Nevermind all that, you kill Lacassine and there will be no war."

Fortier was certain now that he was in the company of a foolish old man, but looking into his eyes, he sensed determination that matched his own.

"You want me kill Lacassine?" he asked the old man.

"Yes," the old Ishak answered, "I will help you."

"Why?" a confused Fortier asked.

The old man seemed to lose himself in deliberation for a long moment before he answered. His words then came slow and soft.

"I will tell you this, for we go to deaths door together. I do not wish to speak of this ever again."

Suffering was etched into the old man's face when he spoke and Fortier felt that the old warrior had never spoken of this to anyone before. He felt pity for the Ishak from the start of his confession.

"Long ago, I was a sub-chief of the village I lived in. I took a woman and we were content. Not long after the spirits gave my woman a child, a party of Opelousa attacked our village. There was a short but vicious battle and the Opelousa were driven off. I was young and I had never seen a battle."

The old man looked directly into Fortier's eyes. The Frenchman could see the pain the old warrior had endured like an image reflecting back at him.

"During the battle, I stayed in my hut with my woman and child."

Fortier looked away with embarrassment, but the old man edged closer and continued.

"I was scorned by the villagers; my woman told me to leave her hut, for it was no longer mine."

The old man paused for a moment and then continued in a quiet rage.

"Lacassine was responsible for the death of the woman that was once mine and now I will earn her respect, even though she is part of the world above. I will avenge her by helping kill Lacassine."

Fortier sat forward with a sharp intake of breath as the realization hit him.

"Your woman was..." he blurted.

"Yes," the old man said, "Soco was my woman. Kata is my child."

Fortier shook his head and slowly tried to digest this sudden, unbelievable news. But it was not unbelievable, it all fit in. The aging, nearby protector of Soco and Kata had been there for a reason. The Frenchman clapped a hand on the old man's lean shoulder and said, "Let us make plans, Yok."

Two days had passed since Yok had found Fortier. The weather had gone from cool and humid to cold and wet. Showers fell intermittently every day. It was usually a light chilly rain but on two occasions the wind had risen to a squall and the rain had fallen in deluge.

The inclement weather had not hampered the determination of the two men. Yok had made the Frenchman rid himself of the buckskin shirt and trousers he wore and these had been replaced with the breechcloth common to Ishak men. Fortier kept a hide wrapped about himself constantly. He noticed that the old Indian only wore his own hide when the wind howled, and he marveled at Yok's immunity to the frigid, humid weather.

The brogans Fortier had worn had been replaced with a pair of deerskin moccasins. The Frenchman had been impressed with the simplicity of their construction when the old man had fashioned them. He had cut the outline of Fortier's feet from a piece of skin and sewed two seams, one up the front and one up the back. He had then used his fishbone needle to sew a flap of skin that wrapped around the ankle and was tied securely. It was very simple, but practical.

The pair moved constantly from one location to another and Fortier knew they could not be going directly to Lacassine's village. This and the fact that the Frenchman had no idea as to where they were caused him to question the old man about his intentions and their location.

"You are learning much more than where you are," the old man had answered. "You are learning what you must know to succeed."

As they moved slowly westward, the broad, flat prairies disappeared. They encountered mostly marshland and the Frenchman was sure that no white man would ever want this land. Some of the more daring trappers may come here for pelts, but they would never bring their families here.

After a long mornings walk, Yok halted them at the first dry patch of land they had seen that day. It was a small plateau surrounded by marsh with a small pond at its center.

"We will stay here tonight and talk," Yok said. "You can see where the marsh ends and the forest begins again, there to the west. Lacassine's village is only a short walk into the forest."

Fortier felt a stir of anxiety at these words. He set his pack down and walked to the small pond. Crouching, he scooped a hand through the water and drank thirstily. He instantly spit the water from his mouth and gagged as his stomach tightened. The thick liquid was heavy brine that left a bitter taste in the Frenchman's mouth.

Fortier turned and noticed Yok smiling. After a moment of hacking coughs, he found his voice.

"Why you not tell?"

"The next time you see a salt pond," Yok said, "You will recognize it before you drink."

Fortier finally managed a smile when be had succeeded in spitting the bitter taste from his mouth.

"You get salt here?" Fortier asked.

"From a place like this one," Yok said. "I put the water in clay pots and set them in the sun. When the water goes to the clouds, I have a pot of salt."

As they set about making themselves as comfortable as possible for the night, Fortier thought of all the old man had taught him in the past two days. Some of the lessons had been harsh, and most of them had been hurried. The Frenchman found it strange that practically all of them had been lessons about the land, and how to survive and adapt to it. He found it hard to fathom how that knowledge could help him in his quest to kill Lacassine.

Seated wrapped in their hide blankets, with no fire, the two munched corn quietly.

"When will you show me how to kill Lacassine?" Fortier asked, once again using some words and much sign. "You have been teaching me about living in this land, as Chaoui did."

As the words left his lips, Fortier felt a strong pang of remorse. The old man read this in his face and, clasping the Frenchman's hand, spoke gently.

"Do not grieve for Chaoui. He did only what he felt he must do. Many times in our lives our actions are dictated by the wishes of someone else. If Chaoui chose to give Kata what she wished, that was his choice. Just as I am choosing to give Soco what she always wished, and you are choosing to risk death for whatever reason you truly feel. He made his choice, just as we have made ours."

Once again, Fortier could only shake his head at the old man's wisdom.

"I did not know," Fortier said, "how much danger Chaoui was facing when he stood for me. I would like to know how he stopped Nementou and the villagers from punishing me when the children were lost on the great water."

The old man chuckled heartily at these words. Fortier sat staring inquisitively and the old man explained.

"Chaoui did much to save you, but he did not save you from Nementou's council of decision. Soco was responsible for saving you."

"I did not know Soco spoke to Nementou," Fortier said.

"She did not," Yok continued. "You see, Soco never had any problem controlling Nementou. She always said that Chaoui should have been chief for Nementou was honest, but rather dense when decisions were required. She said that if he could just once stop trying to emulate his dead father, he might become a good chief for the Vermilion Band."

"Soco simply had me approach Nementou at the ceremonial pole and tell him that the two boys had been taken from our village by the spirits in exchange for the two Opelousa children that he had killed before you came here. I told him that the spirits did not approve of making war on children, and that we had lost Choc's sons because of his, Nementou's, hate. As Soco had predicted, Nementou's decision was made for him."

Fortier was amazed by the events that had taken place right before him, that he had missed entirely. He sat musing until darkness was fully upon them, all the while, slightly aware of Yok's chanting.

"The time has come, so listen carefully," Yok said as he ended his prayers. "You go to kill shaman, so you must do this in the Ishak way. I will show you the site of Lacassine's village and then I will leave you. For four days you must be alone. You must pray to an animal spirit that appeals to you for his help."

"At the end of this time, you must go to Lacassine's hut in the darkness and kill him. "If you succeed without discovery, I will be near the village and will lead you back to your people. If you are discovered and killed, I will walk into the village as a friendly visitor and kill Lacassine when he greets me."

Fortier knew that neither of them stood any chance of survival. Even if his younger years enabled him to slip into the hut of the shaman and kill him unnoticed, they would surely be caught. The slow pace of Yok would prevent them from escaping the avenging villagers. If he killed Lacassine and was apprehended before he left the village, the warriors would still probably search the surrounding area for accomplices. Yok's age would deny him the chance of escape.

The Frenchman merely nodded to all of Yok's plans and accepted his fate stoically. Yok rose and motioned for Fortier to follow him. Entering the forest, they approached a small stream and moved along the gurgling water silently. Deep into the thick hardwood they came upon a large mound that appeared white and glowing in the darkness. Fortier at once discerned that this was the midden, the huge pile of waste from the village. All Ishak camps seemed to have them, and their white glow derived from the fact that they were comprised mainly of clam and oyster shells.

Yok signaled silence and pointed up the stream. Fortier could see fires burning and thought he recognized huts in the darkness. Looking harder, he could definitely see two huts that were elevated higher than the fires. He knew these to be the chief's hut and the hut of the shaman, which were always built on mounds higher than the rest of the village.

Yok allowed him a while to study the village in the limited visibility and then signaled they move back. When they were some distance from the village, he motioned in sign for Fortier to move into a thicket and pray. He produced a small pouch of dried corn and handed it to the Frenchman.

"Eat only this corn for the four days of your ceremony," Yok whispered. "I will not be far, but you must not seek me out. You must see no one. On the night of the fourth day, go and do what you must."

Fortier knew that the old man's bow would serve him no purpose at such close quarters as he hoped to gain, and he was content with his knife. His proficiency with the bow was limited anyway. The Frenchman smiled at the old man, trying desperately to hide his grim mood. Yok merely nodded in response.

Fortier turned into the heavy thicket and quietly worked his way in. The old man stood staring at the place Fortier had entered the thicket for a long time after the Frenchman was gone. He muttered a few words to himself and retrieved his belongings that had been set aside. He turned and set out as fast as he could move, in the direction from which they had come.

# CHAPTER 9

❀

*F*ortier awoke with a start. He knew instantly that he had been asleep and some sound of movement had awakened him. He gazed about slowly and, in his peripheral vision, saw the rabbit move away. He began to switch his position to allow sleep to overcome him again, but a mild stomach cramp completely awakened him. His corn was gone and, although the pallet he had constructed of palmettos was comfortable, he was tired of this vigil.

On the first day he had thought of Kata, fought the guilt of Chaoui's death, and felt the fear and foolishness of being where he was until he had forced all thought from his mind.

The second day found him trying desperately to pray as Yok had instructed and conjure up some form of vision, to no avail. The apprehension of his task ahead would continually spoil his concentration.

Now, on this third day, he was attempting to suppress his thoughts with sleep. He was in need of a meal, but he had certainly not been denied rest, so sleep would not come.

When darkness fell he moved out of the tangled growth of shrub and vines and began walking slowly toward the village. He would stop every ten steps and listen to the sounds of the night.

Halfway to the village he stopped and sat near a large hickory tree. Knowing there was every probability he would die this night, he experienced a wave of regret for so little accomplished in his lifetime. It seemed it had only really begun when he had been brought to Nementou's village. It had been short, but he did find some contentment in knowing that he had loved and been loved.

He rose and continued to the village. He approached it slowly from the same place that he and Yok had observed it from three nights past. He looked carefully about himself, wondering where the old man may be. He saw and heard nothing nearby, so shrugging his shoulders; he fell to a crouch and moved on.

Nearing the camp, he could hear voices and his breathing quickened. He was grateful that the two elevated huts and all of the common huts were on his side of the bayou. The water in the stream had risen perceptively from two nights past and he was happy that he did not have to swim to the village.

There was only one hut between him and the raised huts and Fortier could see no one near this structure. Straining his eyes into the darkness, he saw a drying rack for meat standing between the common house and the two higher ones. He fell to a crawl and moved slowly behind the rack. There was no one near, but he knew that to dash up the mounds to the two huts would leave him exposed for a long time. Even in the darkness, some glancing eye may encounter his running form and raise alarm.

On the far side of the two huts he could see a small, cleared field that was probably used for growing corn. Beyond the field was forest. He quickly decided to try to move behind the mounds since it was unlikely that anyone would be in the field at this hour.

Fortier tensed all of his muscles and held his breath as he prepared to dash for the field. He glanced one last time to the center of the camp where be could see four warriors sitting near a large fire. He did not know the size of the village and, although Yok had said it was larger than Nementou's village, he hoped most of the inhabitants had been driven inside of the huts by the cold.

Just as he was ready to jump into a run, something caused him to look at the fire again. He stared for a moment at the warriors sitting there and then looked down at himself. He looked back at the Indians and slowly, a grin formed on his face.

The dirt of the thicket, alligator oil, and days of having his skin exposed to the elements had turned his complexion to a leathery brown hue. The loincloth and moccasins given to him by Yok had transformed Fortier into a man that, from a distance, would appear quite similar to the warriors seated near the fire. The only disadvantage was his beard, but in this darkness…?

The Frenchman held his breath and rose slowly. He turned his head away from the center of the village and began to walk slowly to the rear of the mounds. As he walked he looked quickly at the front of the elevated huts and noticed a tangle of bones over the door of one. He let his breath out slowly when he reached the rear of the mounds. A rush of panic went through him suddenly when he heard the voices of the men at the fire rise for a moment. He was on the verge of bolting into the trees when the tone subsided to its previous level. He went up the mound of the shaman's hut in a crouch and molded himself to its rear wall. Yok had told him to look for the bones over the door, so he was sure he was behind the correct house.

The only entrance was the door on the opposite side, so Fortier moved slowly along its wall. When he came to the side of the hut nearest the village center he stopped. He could see the fire now and he noticed that there were only three men seated there now. He was about to reverse his progress when he saw the fourth man standing near a tree not far from the fire. The man was urinating and Fortier stared until he was certain that it was the same man that had been seated at the fire. His fear began to mount to terror. He did not trust his courage to prevent him from running, even though he had come this far.

Without any further thought, he took four quick steps and went through the hide hanging over the door. The knife was in his hand as he fell into the hut and quickly sprang to his feet. There was little light in the shaman's abode, but enough to enable Fortier to know he was alone.

A red, eerie glow came from the oyster shell fireplace in the center of the hut. He felt his stomach tighten from fear as he gazed about. It was profoundly the most evil and diabolical appearing place the Frenchman had ever seen.

The walls were covered with snakeskins and feathers; baskets lined the floor filled with shells of odd shapes. Near the shaman's sleeping pallet were two large baskets that were covered by hide blankets. Fortier moved in a soundless crawl to these baskets and quickly removed one of the hide blanket covers. He felt his flesh crawl as the human skulls stared up at him from the grisly container. It was filled with bones that could only be human. He raised the blanket from the second basket only enough to know that this one held the same contents. He felt the same terror that he had experienced when the village of Ishak had screamed of his capture.

"Savages," he muttered to himself. He looked about and chose an advantage point in the hut to strike from when the shaman entered. He moved to just inside of the hide door covering and settled down to wait.

Moments after he stationed himself he heard the hide pulled aside. He gripped the knife so that his knuckles shone white and he prepared to spring.

A moment passed and the hide fell back into place. No one entered and Fortier's mind began to scream and his hands began to shake. As he struggled to control himself, he heard a voice from outside of the hut.

"This is forbidden! Who is in the house of Lacassine? Come out of my temple."

Fortier was bewildered. He glanced around and saw the evidence directly in line with the entrance. The hide blanket he had pulled from the basket of bones lay on the ground two steps from the container. Just a glance from where he crouched, or from someone entering the hut told that it could not have fallen that far.

As he cursed himself for his oversight, the voice called again.

"Come out or I will burn the hut."

He began to hear many voices raised in uproar outside of the door. He considered his chance of running out and trying to surprise the villagers, in order to gain the time to move to Lacassine and plunge the knife into him. He realized the hopelessness of this for he did not know Lacassine. The shaman's headdress would reveal him but Fortier knew he would not have that much time. He dropped the knife and walked out of the door expecting to die instantly.

The torchlight was crowded with faces staring at him in disbelief. He recognized instantly the head-dress of a shaman and the stout man wearing it spoke with authority.

"Who are you?"

The expression on the face of Lacassine, the gaping mouths of the women and the hostile stares from the warriors wrought mild hysteria in the Frenchman.

"An Ishak with a beard," Fortier answered.

Many of the villagers moved back a bit but Lacassine began to smile. Looking at the smile, Fortier wished he had not left the knife in the hut.

"I could have killed you," Fortier whispered.

The shaman and the Frenchman stared at one another with burning hatred for a moment and then Lacassine spoke.

"Tie him by the fire."

Fortier was taken roughly to the center of the village and bound to stakes embedded in the ground. He could hear Lacassine speaking loudly to the villagers, telling them who this strange person was. He closed his eyes and ears and began to pray that Yok did not fail as well, just as the blows began to rain down upon him.

A scream pierced the darkness and Fortier opened his eyes. He realized that he had been unconscious for an undetermined time. While he had been gone from reality he had dreamed, seeing himself kneeling on the banks of the Cata-Oula and praying.

When his vision cleared the pain hit him in a swift wave. His entire body was bruised and battered from the constant pounding the villagers had inflicted. He was still staked to the ground and his field of vision was limited. The hapless Frenchman arched his back to see to his rear and noticed the majority of the village clustered together and staring solemnly at the hut of the chief. Once again, the scream that had awakened him crashed through the stillness. As it erupted, a body somersaulted from the door of the chief's hut and rolled to the bottom of the hill on which the house was situated.

Fortier did not recognize the Indian that curled into the fetal position as soon as he completed his fall. He stared at the crowd of villagers with panic filled eyes on the verge of madness. The Frenchman saw Lacassine and an Indian he assumed was the village chief step from the hut at the top of the hill, followed by two warriors.

Lacassine leaned and whispered to the chief and after a moment the chief spoke.

"This miserable Opelousa is a hunter for the white devils. Because of this, he is more terrible than the whites. He has aided them in bringing about the end of our old ways and this makes him our enemy."

Fortier could almost feel the breathing of the crowd quicken as they all inched closer to the Opelousa captive. He expected to see anger in their faces, but could only detect a crazed fanaticism.

The chief turned to enter his hut but stopped before he did so. He swung around dramatically, pointed to the Opelousa and yelled.

"He is yours for ceremony!"

The crowd exploded forward with screams of frenzy. They lifted the Opelousa and carried him to within ten meters of Fortier. The men began to chant in a hypnotic monotone, while the women continued to scream. The Opelousa was forced to his hands and knees while two villagers restrained him. He turned to the Frenchman and muttered an unintelligible word that was cut short by the two warriors holding him.

Their knives descended in unison, hacking at the man's neck. Fortier felt hot bile rise into his throat as the Opelousa' head fell to the ground and rolled to within centimeters of his own. The villager's chants and screams rose in volume as they danced around the decapitated corpse. Fortier began to pray out loud to his God for now he was sure these Ishak did not have one.

He checked an urge to withdraw into whimpering as the same two hacking warriors sliced off the dead man's arms. The villagers all carried a piece of bone and once the arms were removed, they all converged on the mutilated Opelousa. As one, they began to stab and claw at the body. Fortier turned his gaze from the atrocity and could not stop his flow of tears. Slobbering sounds drew his attention and when he looked, a sour, dry retch erupted from his parched throat. Some of the men were eating the raw fat from the open corpse while others pulled strips of flesh loose and stuffed it into baskets. The women continued to dance and scream, waving pieces of bone over their heads. The last thing Fortier heard before he sank into unconsciousness was his own scream join those of the feasting cannibals.

# CHAPTER 10

*T*he Frenchman awoke to rough handling. Morning had broken, cold and gray, and he could see no evidence of the horror he had witnessed the night before. A light rain was falling and Fortier whispered a silent prayer of thanks that the incessant screaming had stopped.

"No amount of rain," he mumbled, "can cleanse what I have seen here."

One of the braves clubbed him with the back of his hand after releasing him from the stakes and lifting him from the ground.

"Beat me senseless, you devil," Fortier said weakly, "so I cannot feel your inhuman feeding."

He was taken to the place that the unfortunate Opelousa had been condemned. The villagers gathered about and the Frenchman fought to suppress the terror that consumed him.

It seemed an eternity before the shaman and chief emerged from the chief's hut. Something inside the white man pleaded with his rational side to beg for his life. But this sensation was accompanied by the vision of Chaoui in the ground and a shaven-headed Kata staring with unseeing eyes.

"The Cannouche will die today," Fortier heard the chief say. "Lacassine and three warriors will take him to the clearing. His body will be hung from a tree as a warning to any whites coming into our land."

The Chief returned to his hut as Lacassine descended the hill. When Fortier noticed the grin on the shaman's face he began to struggle for the chance to reach the madman.

"Why you not eat me too, you devil?" Fortier yelled.

Lacassine stopped before the Frenchman and fixed him with a withering stare.

"What did you say?" the shaman asked.

"You only eat Opelousa? Not white men?" Fortier said, struggling.

"Silence the fool," Lacassine said, shaking his head.

Fortier was immediately clubbed to the ground. In a state of semi-consciousness, Fortier felt himself being carried away from the village. He knew that he must have lost consciousness, for what seemed like moments later, he found himself sitting against a tree in a clearing that he remembered as being some distance from the village. Just beyond the small clearing he could see one side of the thicket where he had performed his praying ritual. Perhaps he had not prayed long enough; he should have followed Yok's instructions better.

The braves were standing idly by, watching as a tall warrior positioned himself before the Frenchman. Lacassine spoke to his three accomplices.

"Rather than leave the white man here, our Chief should have had us throw his bones into the bayou so that his remains would wash away from our land."

He then nodded to the tall warrior who then drew his war club from the waistband that held it. Fortier closed his eyes and whispered, "Kata, forgive me; you were right."

The Frenchman heard a hollow thunk and felt the hot liquid wash over his face. Funny, he thought, there is so little pain. He opened his eyes and realized why. The tall warrior standing before him was clutching at his throat, trying desperately to dislodge the arrow protruding from it. The projectile had evidently severed the Indian's jugular for the man's blood was gushing onto Fortier. The warrior fell to his knees with a childlike whimper as Lacassine and the two remaining warriors swept the clearing with their eyes.

The three Ishak and Fortier noticed the small, frail-looking figure of Yok at the opposite end of the clearing. The old man dropped his bow and drew a knife as an ancient war cry rang across the open space.

"Bring him to me," Lacassine hissed to his two warriors.

"Run Yok, Lacassine is here!" Fortier yelled.

The shaman spun around and pulled a knife from beneath his blanket.

"You and the old fool will die together," the furious shaman spat.

Fortier and Lacassine both looked to where the two warriors had almost closed on Yok. Fortier began to lower his eyes when a chorus of war yells broke across the clearing. Nementou, Katash and three other warriors emerged from the trees at a fast run. A wave of arrows felled the two warriors near Yok, and the old man began to run toward Fortier and Lacassine. The shaman reached for the tall, dead executioners' bow and this enabled Fortier to lunge from the tree. He vaulted into the shaman and they fell to the ground in a crash of flailing arms and legs. Fortier pounded the shaman's face with his little remaining strength while Lacassine choked the white man furiously. The Frenchman's strength diminished and his arms fell limply to his sides. The shaman leaned over to retrieve the knife that had flown aside when they fell and Yok's yell rang out nearby.

"Lacassineeeee!"

The shaman rose to meet the rush of the old man and they came together with a thud. Shaman and old one, fanatic and wise man, wild man and coward. They stood pressed against one another for a brief moment, and Fortier raised himself to his elbows. Nementou and his warriors ran up to the scene and all witnessed the two Ishak fall to the ground.

Lacassine's features were twisted in the grimace of death and Yok's eyes were fluttering when they separated them. Fortier crawled to the side of the old man and held his head.

The old man's vision seemed to clear momentarily and when he saw Fortier, a smile lined his wrinkled face. He spoke to the Frenchman in a whisper.

"I am dead, you must be Yok now."

The Frenchman heard Nementou giving orders to the warriors. He looked up and Nementou addressed him.

"Come, Yok is gone to the place above. We must hurry from this evil place."

When Fortier attempted to rise, he collapsed to the ground unconscious.

Nementou's hut was spacious. Fortier looked about and realized this for the first time in the two days that he had been here. Of course for most of that time he had slept, so it was no wonder he had not been observant.

On two occasions he could remember being fed a hot liquid by a woman. He had been sure that it was Kata until his swimming senses had cleared and he recognized Patassa, Nementou's woman. On this third morning, he felt much better, only weak.

He rose from the sleeping pallet and emerged from the hut. The village looked much the same, only drearier because of the overcast sky. When he walked down from the hut he saw Kata sitting outside of her hut fashioning a basket. Looking close, he realized it was the type used by the women to cradle infants. When she noticed Fortier she lowered her eyes, and as he walked toward her, he was intercepted by Nementou.

"Come, we must speak," the Chief said.

Fortier followed Nementou back to the hut in silence. The Frenchman felt many stares directed their way and decided not to return any of them. They entered the hut and sat facing one another across the fireplace.

"It is too soon to approach Kata," Nementou said. "If you wish to remain here, you may speak to her in time, but for now, it is too soon."

Fortier nodded his understanding. Strange, he thought, he had always felt uncomfortable in the presence of Nementou and now for some reason, he did not. He found himself staring at the chief and checked himself.

"Is it too soon for me to ask what happened?"

"No," Nementou said, 'I asked you here to tell you this."

He paused for a moment and Fortier noticed a new glimmer of self-confidence in the Chief's manner.

"When Kata returned to the village and told of what had happened in the forest, I knew that I had been wrong to wish to surrender you to Lacassine. I should have known that Chaoui would never allow this."

When Nementou said Chaoui's name, both men saw a flicker of despair and guilt flash across the other's eyes. When Nementou spoke again, his voice was still full of confidence, but laced with a sadness.

"Hearing of Chaoui's death, for three days I sat in my hut and all I could think of were my own weaknesses. If I had not killed the Opelousa children, Choc would not have lost his sons. If I had not brought you here, Chaoui would not have had to die protecting you for my folly. If I had not spent so much time trying to decide what my father would have done in these situations, I may have had an easier time filling his position as it should have been filled."

"I decided to do everything I could to right my wrongs, in Chaoui's honor. I ordered four of my warriors to join me in preparation for battle. We began our four day ritual of prayer and at its end we embarked for Lacasaine's village."

"Soon after we left our village, we encountered Yok. He bad been traveling at great haste and he was very weary. Earlier, here in our village, he had heard Kata's words and set out immediately to kill Lacassine. He always did have some special fondness for the girl, her mother and Chaoui. He told us of how he had encountered you and that you were on a mission similar to ours. He knew that he could not stop you from your attempt so he stalled your actions until he could return here and plead to me for help. He did not know that I had already made my decision to avenge Chaoui."

"Why did he return for you?" Fortier asked. "Why did he no have us try kill Lacassine alone?"

"He knew that if he would not return for help from me that you would both die. For some reason of his own, he wanted to keep you alive."

"He was a Chief," Fortier whispered, releasing a long sigh.

For a while, both men sat staring into the fireplace.

"I have sent two warriors," Nementou said, "to retrieve the body of Chaoui. He will have a proper burial."

Fortier realized that Nementou would be burying both his brother and his father with this action and remained silent with his thoughts. After an extended pause, Fortier broke the reverie.

"When I can speak to Kata?"

"I will inform you as to when you may speak to my dead brother's wife," Nementou answered brusquely.

For an intense moment, the two men looked into each other's eyes.

"Nementou," Fortier said quietly. "I never dishonor your brother."

After several moments a slow smile crept onto Nementou's face.

"No, you did not, Hiyen. You helped avenge him."

The two men rose and walked to the door of the hut. They emerged and stood looking over the village.

"Will warriors from Lacassine's village come?" Fortier asked quietly.

"We removed all evidence of our presence," Nementou said. "The chief of that village was never very clever, that is why he was always Lacassine's tool. They will probably think that spirits or white men killed Lacassine and his warriors and whisked you away."

Some of the villagers looked up at them for a moment and then went about their work. Kata's look lingered on them for a moment longer than the rest, and then she continued her chore.

"We will move soon," Nementou said, "for the buffalo will be coming to the prairies northwest of here."

"Do you wish for me to inform the people?" Fortier asked hesitantly.

Nementou turned to the Frenchman and looked deep into his eyes for a long moment.

"Yes, go and do that Hiyen."

Fortier began walking down the hill but stopped midway, turned to his Chief and announced loudly.

"I am now called Yok."

# CHAPTER 11

The buffalo moon was upon the land of the Ishak. The cold, blustery winds that were usually accompanied by rain swept often through the village. Five days previous, when Fortier had spread word through the encampment that it was time to move, he had not realized that the move was an annual migration of sorts for Nementou's band. He had learned since that this village was only a small part of the Ishak. There was still much about the tribe that Fortier did not know, and he had questioned Nemtentou about the winter migration.

Nementou had explained that the Hiye Kiti or Sunrise People of the Ishak usually spent spring and summer near the coast of the great water. They would split into small bands that had little trouble affording itself food from the abundance of fish, shellfish and wild plants of which the coastal area teemed. When the Great Corn Moon waned and the frigid temperatures of winter visited upon the land, the Hiye Kiti moved inland, congregated, hunted, and waited for spring.

To Fortier's surprise the people of the village had not shunned him or treated him as he had expected upon his return. The drowned boys were not mentioned by anyone. The flight from Lacassine, the death of Choc, Chaoui and Yok, and even the retaliatory killing of the great shaman seemed forgotten. Just as Fortier seldom heard any of the people speak of the dead; these episodes seemed erased from the minds of the people.

Fortier was treated by everyone in the village as common as if he had been born amongst them. By everyone except Kata. He had not spoken to her since his return.

After three days Nementou had informed him that he was at liberty to do as he pleased in the encampment. He was no longer a slave; his act of courage had earned him warrior status. His one attempt to speak to Kata had left him confused and hurt. She had looked through him as if he did not exist and not answered or even acknowledged his presence. After that miserable failure, he had grown uncomfortable in her presence and intentionally avoided her.

As the village went through the final preparations before departure, Fortier helped Nementou's woman, Patassa, strap vines over their belongings on the travois that would be pulled by two of the village dogs. Nementou joined them after giving instruction as to the order of travel, and once again Fortier was impressed with the change in the Chief's appearance and manner.

Nementou exuded confidence and looked nothing short of regal in his winter attire. His buffalo robe was painted red on the inside with attractive designs etched in black. The buffalo tail had been left on the hide and as it trailed behind the Chief, Fortier was reminded of pictures of the long robes of kings that he had seen.

"It appears we are ready to begin," Nementou announced.

"How far is this journey?" Fortier asked of the Chief.

"We Hiye Kiti and some Hikike will meet at the river we call Calcasieu. That is about a three-day walk from here, but we will take longer. I wish to stop and trade with the Avoyels."

"Are the Hikike also Ishak?" Fortier queried.

Patassa chuckled at the Frenchman's question as Nementou answered.

"The Hikike are the Sunset People of the Ishak. The other tribes call them the Akokisa. We have many relations among them. Soco and Kata were of their band before Kata was chosen by Chaoui as his woman."

The usual silence that always seemed to pass between Fortier and Nementou when Chaoui was mentioned once again descended. The people of the village were giddy with the anticipation of the journey that would reunite relatives and perhaps begin new relationships, but the Chief and the Frenchman walked at the head of the small entourage despondent with their grief and guilt.

As the Vermilion Band moved northwest towards their destination, the forest became a high, open prairie. On the second day of travel, the land became small rolling hills covered with pine forests.

Fortier's command of the language of the Ishak became more proficient as each day passed. His conversations with Nementou as they walked at the head of the column helped the hours of travel go quickly. Theirs was not the happy and excited buzz of chatter from the people that followed them, but they both discovered that they enjoyed each other's company.

Occasionally, Fortier would look back to where Kata walked with an old woman known as Yuk' hiti. The two women had been spending much time together and it seemed Yuk' hiti was often counseling Kata. Fortier found that whenever Kata noticed him glancing back, she would immediately lower her eyes. He decided that the pain of her rejection was as difficult to bear as the grief of Chaoui's death. He knew there was no easy solution to this dilemma, so he bore it stoically. He knew that this was probably exactly how poor Yok had lived his life and he felt a wave of sympathy for the old warrior. The old man had been braver than anyone had known.

When the band stopped to make camp for the second night, Fortier sat with Nementou as Patassa quickly constructed a rough lean-to of poles and hides for sleeping. They munched persimmons from their nearly depleted supply and conversed quietly as the camp prepared for sleep.

"When morning comes, I will go to an Avoyel camp that is near here to trade," Nementou said. "You and Katash will come with me. The people will wait here and we will continue our journey when we return."

"What will this trade be?" Fortier asked.

"At this time of year," Nementou chuckled, "the only thing we have left to trade is smoked fish. The Avoyels like smoked fish though, so we should fare well."

"What will we get for our fish?"

"Flint, of course," Nementou said matter-of-factly. "The Avoyels are the flint people. Most of the tribes get their flint from them."

"Nementou," Fortier said, "Have you not considered trading some of our goods for muske…firesticks?"

"This is the second time I have been asked that question," Nementou answered thoughtfully. "Many tribes are trading for many of the white man's goods. Even some Ishak; Kinimo of the Teche Band has a fondness for white man's things. I suppose he has firesticks by now. I feel that if we do start to use the white man's tools and weapons that we will quickly lose the old ways of our people. Lacassine was a madman but there was some truth to some of his ravings. I fear that our children's children may have many decisions to make concerning the white man and his goods."

"As you wish, Nementou," Fortier answered as he curled into his tattered buffalo robe for sleep.

He drifted off sure of two thoughts. One, that the decisions Nementou spoke of would have to be made long before his children's children were ever born, and two, that he did not want to be the one to make Nementou aware of this.

Fortier and Nementou stepped easily along on the forest floor of scented pine needles. The trade at the Avoyel village had gone well. Their bartered sack of flints, in spite of its value, was easy to tote in comparison to the three bundles of smoked fish that they had carried enroute to the Avoyel camp.

Fortier had easily been able to follow the negotiation Nementou conducted for he had utilized the hand signs to communicate. Although the Frenchman was unfamiliar with the barter terms of these people, upon departure from the Avoyel village, Katash had complemented Nementou on his shrewd tactics. Fortier felt an unfamiliar sense of pride in his Chief's accomplishment.

The pair ambled along, expecting at any moment to catch sight of Katash. The village tracker had gone ahead to attempt to find an easier crossing of a swollen bayou that the trio had forded that morning.

"We are near the flooded bayou that wet our robes," Nementou said, stopping. "Let us wait here for Katash and hope that he has discovered a better crossing."

"Do you trade with anyone else besides the Avoyels?" Fortier asked, seating himself on a fallen tree.

"We trade much more often with the Chitimachas than with the Avoyels. We can usually acquire enough flint for an entire season in one trade, so we do not visit the Avoyels often. However, the Chitimachas make fine eating and cooking containers that our women admire, so we visit and trade with them very often."

Fortier shifted uncomfortably on the log, and Nementou detected an unease in him. Before the Chief could ask the Frenchman what bothered him, Fortier spoke.

"Nementou, I fear that Kata holds me responsible for Chaoui's death."

The Chief inhaled with an audible gasp, his eyes boring into the Frenchman. He started to speak twice before the right words would come to him.

"Yok, you and I have spoken of his death many times and yet it does not become any easier to bear. Kata and I have spoken, and I do not believe what you suspect is true. When Ouaron and Escanimon returned with Chaoui's body, I saw the pain and suffering in you. I saw the same in Kata. I think that the three of us blame ourselves for his death. That, we must each deal with on our own. You and Kata have a more difficult responsibility to bear, for you must both deal with the love you have for each other as well as the guilt you each feel because of Chaoui's death. No, you are mistaken Yok. Kata does not blame you. You blame yourself. We will all learn to live with his loss in time. I will not make the same mistake with Chaoui's memory that I made with my fathers."

Fortier did his best to hide his surprise. He had had no idea that Nementou knew of his feelings for Kata. Was it that evident? And could Nementou be right about Kata having feelings for him? How could Nementou think that, after Kata's intentional avoidance of him?

"Nementou," Fortier pleaded, "Kata has not spoken to me or looked at me since I returned. I do not think she is dealing with her feelings for me, I think she is blaming me."

"Poor Yok," Nementou said, shaking his head. "You have so much yet to learn. You see, Kata is carrying Chaoui's child. Women are usually isolated in the birthing hut during this time and may have no contact with anyone but the birthing woman. It is not possible for Kata to be isolated because of our journey, but she must still refrain from contact."

"So Yuk' hiti is the birthing woman?" an enlightened Fortier asked.

"Yes," Nementou said, smiling. "She advises and instructs Kata at the things she must know when the time of birth arrives."

"I feel like a fool," Fortier lamented. "When will I ever learn all that I must know to be Ishak?"

"Give yourself time, Yok. I will continue the training that Chaoui and old Yok began. Someday you may even be a war chief yourself," Nementou added, smiling.

All at once a panting, anxious Katash emerged from the trees at a fast run and quickly forded the stream. He slid to a stop before Nementou and stammered his dire message between deep, choking breaths.

"Tunica…war…party…I found their abandoned encampment. I followed their path. I found evidence that they had observed our own encampment from concealment, then moved away to the east. I found them a short run from our camp, painting for battle."

"Did you warn our people?" Nementou asked calmly.

"Yes, Ouaron began defense preparation. We must hurry for I counted fifteen Tunica warriors."

The three men set off at a lope for their encampment. Running abreast, Fortier spoke to Katash without breaking stride.

"Do the Tunicas know you saw them?"

"No," Katash answered. "I am sure they did not know of my presence, and I left no tracks."

"It may help us if they think we are going to be surprised," Fortier wheezed. "We can make plans for that."

"You see, Yok," Nementou said excitedly, "Already you are thinking like a war chief."

Fortier, Nementon and Katash arrived at their encampment and found the villagers anxious and confused. Ouaron and the other six warriors were hastily filling quivers with arrows and erecting crude barricades amongst the temporary lean-to huts. The women and children were clustered in the center of the camp. The children were whimpering from the fear they sensed and the women were busy trying rather unsuccessfully to quiet them. The camp dogs were barking excitedly from the nervous chatter of the men.

Nementou appraised the scene quickly and immediately called for attention.

"Escanimon, gather the women and children and take them away from the camp. Go north and do not stop until you are well away from here. Stay with them until I send for you. If someone does not come for you by morning, continue for the rendezvous at the Calcasieu, traveling as quickly as you can."

The young warrior started to question Nementou's instruction but was silenced by a wave of the Chief's hand. Nementou then instructed the warriors to dismantle the partially assembled barricades and gather at the center of the camp.

Fortier hurried to his travel pack and unwrapped Nementou's spare war club. The Chief had recently constructed a new one for himself and the Frenchman knew that he could put this old one to good use. As he turned to move to the center of the camp, he saw Escanimon hurrying the women and children into the forest. Kata and Yuk' hiti were last in the file of non-combatants and Fortier realized that Kata was staring at him. He thought he detected a look of concern on her face, but she quickly turned her head and faded into the trees with the old woman. The Frenchman rushed to the center of the camp where Nementou was detailing a plan.

"The Tunica outnumber us, and we cannot outrun them. We are sure that they do not know that we are aware of their planned attack. Yok has made me remember a village defense that my father once told me of."

Most of the assembled warriors turned to Fortier. The Frenchman was suddenly embarrassed by the nods of approval that he received from all around him.

"We shall make our encampment look as if it is asleep," Nementou continued. "We shall build fires inside of the huts to confuse these Tunica. When they move in to investigate, we shall assault them from the outer edge of the camp, where we will have concealed ourselves."

It was obvious that the warriors approved and had confidence in this strategy, for they immediately moved to the makeshift huts and built small fires within them. They also rolled packs and robes into the forms of sleeping people near the small fires. Darkness was absolute when the nine remaining warriors of the Vermilion Band moved into their positions outside of the camp to wait for the impending attack.

Fortier could just discern the glow of the fires from the position he took within a clump of brush. He listened intently to the night sounds and felt a bead of sweat trickle down the side of his face. He was reminded instantly of his waiting vigil outside of Lacaasine's village and felt a shudder of apprehension. He was momentarily startled as a figure loomed beside him in the darkness. Nementou slithered to his side and whispered quietly.

"Do not move until you hear my war cry. We must surprise them or all is lost. Think of Kata and what these Tunics will do to her; it will make you brave."

Nernentou moved silently off into the night and Fortier was left alone. It seemed an eternity passed without incident and the Frenchman began fighting off the urge to sleep. He knew he was fatigued from the trip back from the Avoyel village and the anxiety and excitement had subsided because of inactivity. He slowly moved his head to look to his right when he heard a slight rustle of leaves from that direction.

In the layers of darkness he detected a movement from a small figure on the ground, not three steps from his position. When he was sure that the figure was that of a small animal, a dim wave of moonlight peeked from behind the evenings cloud cover that Fortier had previously been unaware of. The figure moved to the shadows and Fortier realized he had been looking at a moccasined foot. He struggled to control his rapid breathing as he heard another soft rustle from his left. He grasped the war club in his right hand and his knife in his left until his fingers ached, praying silently.

The Tunica warrior on his left moved between Fortier and the campsite and the Frenchman could see his form clearly silhouetted against the fires from the camp. He slowly turned his head to the right to attempt to locate the first enemy he had seen when Nementou's war cry rang through the forest.

From all around the Frenchman, war cries, shouts of struggle and grunts of pain filled the air. Fortier launched himself from the clump of brush and felt a hard tug at his right shoulder. He tore the branch from where it was lodged behind his right arm and vaulted into the Tunica before him. The warrior grunted in surprise and rolled heavily with the Frenchman. Fortier gained his feet first and swung the heavy war club with all of his strength. The Tunica's head exploded like a melon and Fortier fought back a wave of nausea. He felt rather than saw an arrow whiz by his head from behind the brush in which he had concealed himself. The Frenchman charged the brush and barreled into the Tunica whose moccasin had initially warned Fortier of his presence. The Frenchman felt his knife tear into the warrior's stomach and a hideous scream erupted from the dying Tunica.

Fortier collapsed to the ground embracing the warrior and again fought the violent shivering that attempted to overwhelm him.

When Fortier gained some semblance of control he rose from the ground and scoured the area surrounding him for more enemies. He could see no one and the sounds of battle had subsided. He moved cautiously toward the camp and encountered Katash at the edge of the encampment perimeter. The Ishak signaled that all was well and Fortier exhaustedly walked to join him.

Nementou approached and drawing closer, Fortier noticed the Chiefs hands covered with the blood of his enemies.

"Your plan was a success, Yok," Nementou congratulated.

"It was your plan, Nementou. Or rather, your fathers plan," Fortier whispered with effort.

As he spoke the words, the Frenchman collapsed heavily to the ground. Nementou leaned over him gazing intently.

"Yok tires quickly in battle," Katash said, smiling.

"Help me raise him," Nementou said quickly, "He has taken an arrow."

# CHAPTER 12

❀

*F*ortier awoke to find the villagers preparing to depart from the encampment turned battleground. As he attempted to rise he felt a sharp pain emanate from his right shoulder. Its intensity caused the Frenchman to fall back against the robes he had been lying on, nearly swooning. His exclamation of discomfort brought Katash instantly to his side.

"Remain still, Yok. We will move you to the rendezvous on lodge poles. You have lost much blood."

"What happened to me?" Fortier croaked.

"You were struck by a Tunica arrow. You fell to the ground before any of us knew you were wounded. You fought very well, Yok. Two enemy warriors have gone above because of your bravery."

"Are the Tunicas gone?"

"Yes, we counted four dead and we are sure we wounded at least two others. Ouaron was our only warrior hurt besides you, and his wound is simply a cut to his forearm that will heal quickly. The surprise was complete."

"Is my wound serious?"

"We have cleaned and wrapped it, Yok. We will meet the rest of the Hiye Kiti today. The shaman, Skunnemoke, of the Teche Band will attend to your injury. I am sure he will heal you quickly."

As Katash moved away from the pallet, Fortier felt his head swim from the pain in his shoulder. He prayed for sleep or even unconsciousness, for he did not look forward to being dragged the remainder of the journey over rough terrain by dogs. The pain was practically unbearable lying still. He sensed a presence and opened his eyes to find the old woman, Yuk' hiti kneeling beside him. She offered a bowl of some liquid with downcast eyes. The Frenchman nodded and as the ancient birthing woman brought the bowl to his lips he detected the pungent aroma of herbs.

Fortier gulped the bitter concoction and resisted the inclination to retch by clamping his lips hard. As he lay back against the pallet, he was overcome by dizziness and struggled to speak.

"Thank you, Soco."

The Frenchman was asleep before the words had passed his lips.

Nementou smelled the cookfires of the rendezvous before he could see any of the people gathered there. It was early afternoon and they had made good time on this last part of the journey. Especially considering the fact that they were dragging a wounded warrior in addition to their belongings.

The Chief smiled as he thought of Yok. What a warrior he had become! Almost half of the casualties inflicted on the Tunica war party had been by Yok alone. What a story for Yok to tell around the ceremony campfire. It was good that Yuk' hiti had given him the sleep potion for Yok would have had a hard time on this last day of travel.

The Vermilion Band entered the rendezvous encampment to a chorus of shouts of welcome. It seemed that they were last to arrive as Nementou located the Calcasieu and Teche Bands of the Hiye Kiti and even a small band from the Hikike visiting from far to the west.

As the Vermilion Band moved into the unoccupied space left near the river, Nementou was greeted by Kinimo, Chief of the Teche Band and Ashnoya, Chief of the Calcasieu.

"Welcome Nementou," Kinimo announced. "Ashnoya and I were just wondering if you would arrive today."

An excited chatter erupted from the congregating crowd as they noticed an unconscious white man being pulled by dogs on lodge-poles.

"Is this your same white captive?" Kinimo asked.

"That one has the face hair, but he is not a Cannouche any longer. We were attacked by a war party of Tunica and we repelled them by killing four of their number. Yok there killed two of the four himself. He is an Ishak warrior."

"I think I have seen this Cannouche before," Ashnoya said, stepping forward. "He was in my village during the Turkey Moon."

"Are you sure?" Kinimo asked.

"He looks like the Cannouche that Lacassine and three of my warriors left our village with. They never returned. We found Lacassine and my warriors bloated in the sun."

"If you are sure that this was during the Turkey Moon, then you speak of another Cannouche," Nementou interjected. "Yok has been in our village since the Small Corn Moon."

"He looks the same as the Cannouche we captured in my village," Ashnoya said, staring at Fortier thoughtfully.

"It is easy to understand your mistake, Ashnoya," Nementou said with a laugh. "The Cannouche all look the same to me also."

This elicited a hearty laugh from the people that had gathered around the Chief's conversation. Nementou moved away from the crowd and directed his people to their position near the riverbank. He glanced back at Ashnoya and noticed the Chief take one last hard look at Yok, shake his head and walk to his band's section of the camp. Nementou released a sigh of relief and prayed that Lacassine's spell did not hang over the Calcasieu

Katash sidled up to Nementou and spoke in a low tone.

"It appears Ashnoya was the only one to get a good look at Yok when he was in their village."

"Yes, I imagine the villagers seldom took their eyes off of Lacassine because of their fear of him. And Ashnoya, well, I knew he was easily influenced long before we arrived here."

"You suspected the Calcasieu might recognize Yok?"

"I had prepared my actions in case they did. I was also hoping that with Lacassine gone, Ashnoya would not bother with making an issue of this. It appears that my hopes were granted."

"You handled that situation very well, Nementou. You stopped a serious situation from developing with humor, as your father would have done."

Nementou smiled and shrugged off the compliment.

"Help me Katash. We must take Yok to Skunnemoke's hut."

Fortier saw himself tied to a tree with an arrow protruding from his back. Far to the north, in the distance, he could see a stockade with buckskin-clad men coming and going. The walls of the town were manned by soldiers wearing bright colored uniforms that the Frenchman had never seen before. Lacassine walked by the tree shoving a much-disheveled looking Kata who was carrying a small bundle. They were walking north and Fortier struggled to free himself in spite of the pain from the arrow. He called out to the soldiers to assist him in freeing Kata from the mad shaman, and Lacassine turned and laughed.

"I am taking her to them," Lacassine bellowed.

Fortier's scream rang out desperately, "I will kill you again, Lacassine! I will kill you again Lacassineeeeeee!

The Frenchman opened his eyes to unfamiliar surroundings. Unfamiliar, and yet somehow, familiar. The dark interior instantly brought to mind an evil place he had visited briefly once before. The walls were covered with snakeskins and small animal skeletons. A heavy mist seemed to hang in the air over the hot fire burning in the center of the steaming hovel. He found he was lying on a slightly raised platform of wood covered with moss and skins.

Fortier gasped when a figure materialized from out of the mist and leaned over him. The wrinkled old man wore the head-dress and robes of a shaman and fear hit the Frenchman like a blow. He brought his hands before his face and grunted as the old man offered a bowl of liquid. The shaman made clucking sounds and wiped the sweat from Fortier's brow. He gently offered the bowl of liquid again and Fortier detected no ill intent.

The hot decoction was thick and as red as blood. The Frenchman choked down as much as he could and then lay back gasping. The old man brought forth another bowl that Fortier was happy to find was some form of fish broth that was much easier to digest. When the bowl was empty, the shaman rose and poured water on the coals of the fire that replenished the dissipating steam inside of the hut. He then seated himself at arms length from Fortier and began chanting.

"Who are you, where am I," Fortier whispered.

"I am Skunnemoke of the Teche Band, and you are in the winter camp of the Ishak."

The old man seemed irritated at the interruption of his chanting. He waited until Fortier had eased back into a comfortable position to speak.

"So you killed Lacassine, Um?"

Fortier stared at the old man wide-eyed. His addled mind could perceive no response, so he simply stared.

"I had wondered what could have happened there," Skunnemoke whispered. "I suppose it is no wonder he was killed by a Cannouche."

"I did not kill Lacassine."

"In your dream-speak, you boasted that you would kill Lacassine again."

"I was there when Lacassine was killed," Fortier said, "but I did not kill him. He was killed by an old man called Yok."

"Tell me more of this," the shaman urged.

It took quite an effort for Fortier to relate the story of his capture, his attempt to reach Natchitoches and the events that led to Lacassine's death. He was disoriented from the liquid Skunnemoke had given to him and very weak from his wound. The old man remained silent throughout Fortier's tale. When the Frenchman concluded, the old man urged him to sleep while he prayed.

"Will you send word to Lacassine's village?" Fortier asked sleepily.

"It would not be difficult, they are here."

"Lacassine's people?" Fortier exclaimed, attempting to rise.

"Lay back," the old man insisted, forcing the Frenchman back onto the pallet. "Lacassine's people, as you call them, are the Calcasieu Band. You have nothing to fear from them. It is clear to me now why Nementou persuaded Ashnoya, their Chief, that he had never seen you before. Nementou is the reason you have nothing to fear from the Calcasieu Band."

The old man remained silent for a moment, seemingly lost in his thoughts. After the pause, he shook his head, chuckled, and spoke again.

"He is very clever, that Nementou. Now you hear me out, Cannouche. Yok, the man whose name you now bear, was my friend. I had no special fondness for Lacassine, so this secret is safe with me. I have heard of your deeds and your fondness for the Ishak, so we shall forget about Lacassine. But be aware that if ever I suspect that you are not loyal to the Ishak and are a tool of the Cannouche, I will prove as dangerous to you as Lacassine was. And I will not be easily fooled as Ashnoya was by Nementou."

Fortier relaxed against the pallet; he felt confident that the old man was speaking the truth. He felt an immediate respect and fondness for the old shaman that in many ways reminded him of Yok.

"I will be loyal, Skunnemoke," Fortier whispered, as he eased into sleep. "I intend to be a war chief someday."

The old man shook his head and resumed his chanting.

Fortier emerged from the hut of Skunnemoke and surveyed his surroundings. The winter village was situated along the river Nementou had called Calcasieu in a copse of pine trees adjacent to an open plain. It was a good location for the winter for the young pines formed a barrier to the north, the direction from which they could soon expect cold winds.

For three days the old shaman had administered steaming, pungent potions to the Frenchman, repeatedly cleaned and packed his wound, and chanted constantly over Fortier. The Frenchman had to admit that he felt much better. The sharp pain behind his shoulder had been reduced to a dull ache and Fortier knew that he was well on the way to full recovery.

The size of the village was a surprise to Fortier. He was sure he was looking at well over a hundred huts, and he estimated a population of over two hundred in the winter quarters. When he located a few familiar faces, he moved to join the Vermilion Band at their position near the river.

As he approached he was met by the young brave, Escanimon. The young warrior that had led the women and children away from the battle with the Tunicas looked at Fortier as if in awe.

"May I walk with you, Yok?"

"Of course, Escanimon. "It is good to see you. I am happy to be able to join our band again."

"Yok," the boy began shyly, "I would like to learn to be as fierce a warrior as you. It is hard to imagine besting two enemy warriors in combat, and with no bow. Would you teach me to fight as you do?"

Fortier stopped and stared at the young warrior. It was as strange a moment to the Frenchman as if one of the village dogs had spoken. He had never been looked up to by anyone and had never imagined himself in this situation. He saw the look of insecurity on the boy's face and realized that it had probably taken much courage for the boy to ask this. So rather than crush the image the boy had construed, he merely smiled and nodded.

Escanimon walked excitedly away and joined a group of boys that appeared to be awaiting him. As the group moved away, Fortier could hear Escanimon's words trailing behind him.

"Yes, that's him. He killed two of them with only a knife. He would have killed more, but some coward wounded him from concealment with an arrow. He and I will hunt together…"

What a strange turn of events, Fortier thought. To have been so recently condemned because of the incident on the Gulf and now thought of as some form of hero. He stood there watching the retreating group of boys, lost in his thoughts, when he was joined by Nementou and Katash.

"The women have built a hut for you, Yok," Katash said. "If you find a woman here that you would like for your own, you will have a hut to…offer her."

Fortier and Nementou exchanged glances and Katash felt a silent communication pass between them.

"Have I said something wrong?" a puzzled Katash asked.

"No," Nementou answered, "Yok will have a woman someday, I am sure. Tell us, Yok, has your wound healed?"

"It is fine. It was some experience staying with Skunnemoke. He is a very special man. I am happy I came to know him."

"He is very wise," Nementou offered, "and he is very clever."

"Yes, he is that," Fortier said, "Remind me to tell you of how clever he is sometime when there are not so many people about."

Nementou and Katash looked at the Frenchman inquisitively but before either could speak, Fortier continued.

"When does the hunt begin?"

"After the rendezvous ceremony," Katash said excitedly, "in three days."

"The ceremony does not begin for three days?" Fortier asked.

"The ceremony starts tonight," Nementou explained. "It lasts three days."

"How is that possible?" Fortier exclaimed. "How can a ceremony last for three days?"

"You will see tonight," Nementou said, smiling at Katash.

"It must be some ceremony," Fortier mused.

# CHAPTER 13

*W*hen dusk was upon the Ishak village, Fortier emerged from his hut and joined the warriors of the Vermilion Band to proceed to the ceremonial hut. The Frenchman had slept most of the afternoon, and he had to admit, it was pleasant having ones own hut. He had not been disturbed once, and he felt rejuvenated from the rest.

The ceremonial hut was located between the Vermilion Bands position in the encampment and that of the Teche Band. It was much larger than any of the Chief's huts and Fortier knew that the construction of it must have been a concerted effort by the women of all the bands.

When Nementou and his warriors entered the hut, a respectful moment of silence descended on the men already gathered there. The Vermilion Band's rout of the Tunica war party had earned a new respect for Nementou and his braves, and there were rumors that some young warriors from other bands wished to follow Nementou's group when they left in the spring.

The few women in the hut were busy keeping a fire in the center of the gathering. A large pottery bowl was being hung over the fire as Nementou and his followers filed into position.

From the single door, two women entered carrying a basket of leaves. As they passed Fortier he noticed that the leaves appeared to come from some holly-like plant. The women moved to the large bowl over the fire and placed the leaves into the vessel.

The congregated warriors in the hut began a chatter of anticipation amongst themselves as the leaves quickly toasted over the fire. When the leaves began to parch, one of the women quickly poured water from a container into the bowl.

"Are we to drink this?" Fortier asked of Katash.

"Yes, but not until it boils twice."

The concoction boiled quickly over the roaring fire and as Katash had predicted, after the second boiling, the vessel was removed from the fire. The assembled warriors parted and Skunnemoke walked from the rear of the hut to the large bowl and sprinkled some form of powder into the liquid. His action was accompanied by a few mumbled words that were incomprehensible to the gathering. The attending women quickly poured the hot, yellow liquid into another large bowl to cool.

When the last drops of the ceremonial drink had fallen into the second container, a loud chorus went up from practically every warrior in the hut.

"Who wishes to drink?" rang from the lips of all the men in unison. Fortier noticed that when the shout rang out, the women seemed to freeze in place. They stood as still as statues as the men spoke in low tones to one another.

Two of the men began passing out a number of small bark containers. As the men circulated the hut, one of the containers was mishandled and fell to the ground. One of the women bent to pick up the fallen bowl and a grunt of disapproval rose from the men near this occurrence. The warrior that had dropped the bark container leapt to the fire, pulled a small stick from its base, and proceeded to beat the woman that had moved. The woman retreated from the hut with tears streaming down her face.

"What was that about?" Fortier asked, turning to Nementou with a puzzled look.

"A woman must not move when the ceremonial drink is complete. It could ruin the magic of the drink and we would have to throw it all away."

The men moved in turn to the large vessel, dipping the bark containers into the liquid and drinking deep. Fortier moved to the bowl and noticed that the pouring of the liquid had caused it to become frothy. The liquid was still quite hot and Fortier felt it burn down his throat as he mimicked the warriors that had gone prior to him. The taste and aroma was not unlike tea, but it was thicker and stronger. It did not seem to cause the Frenchman any ill effects and after a few moments he returned to the reforming line of braves desiring more.

The procession continued until the vessel was dry. Fortier had consumed two of the bark containers and found himself wishing for more. As the men began filing from the hut, Katash walked with the Frenchman, and seemed in a jovial frame of mind.

"Do not hurry, Yok. We must wait for the music makers to take their positions."

Fortier felt as if he was floating from the hut and he locked arms with Katash to steady himself.

"There will be music makers?" Fortier slurred.

"Yes, it is time to dance the mitote. I intend to dance until it is time for the hunt," Katash boasted seriously, and then laughed at himself.

A shrill cacophony began from the side of the ceremonial hut and Fortier staggered there to investigate. A group of braves were assembled there playing instruments the Frenchman had never seen. Three of the men played different size flutes or whistles made from reeds, and two others banged primitive tambourines fashioned from turtle shells.

When the Frenchman returned to the center of the village, a large bonfire had been lit and the men had already begun dancing. They circled the fire cavorting wildly, occasionally blurting out monotone phrases concerning the coming of winter.

Fortier suddenly thought of Kata and wondered where she and the other women may be. He walked four paces and then noticed what had to be all of the village women congregated a short distance from the bonfire. They stood together, swaying slowly to the music with their hair covering their faces. Occasionally one of the women would shout some phrase about being thankful for the Great Corn Moon that had recently left them.

The Frenchman walked to within a few paces of the women and stood before them trying to find a familiar form amongst the hair-covered faces.

"Kataaaa" he yelled laughing, trying to be heard over the music and shouting.

"Kataaa, I cannot find you."

Nementou approached Fortier from the fire, took hold of his arm and led him to the prancing group of warriors.

"Dance the mitote, Yok. Dance until it is time for the hunt."

"But the hunt is three days from now," Fortier said, giggling.

"That is right," Nementou said smiling and then launched into the dance.

"I was right," the Frenchman mumbled to himself, "this is some ceremony."

A flock of crows cawing loudly in the large pines near the river awakened Fortier. He opened his eyes and realized he lay against a pile of robes near his hut. It was daybreak, three days since the start of the ceremony and Fortier's head throbbed like a drum. He knew he had lasted until sometime late into the second evening of celebration. His memory was blurred with a confused recall of dancing, chanting and many more trips to new batches of the ceremonial liquid. He knew that most of the warriors had danced on after he had collapsed, for occasionally in his drunken stupor, he would awaken and see that the celebration was still on. He rose slowly and stumbled to his hut, steadying himself against the structure as he reached it.

Nementou emerged from his nearby hut and greeted Fortier warmly.

"Good morning, Yok. Will you soon be ready to depart for the hunt?"

Fortier raised his bloodshot eyes and regarded the Chief incredulously.

"We leave for the hunt soon?" Fortier whispered, his head threatening to burst.

"We leave this morning. The Bear Moon is upon us, Yok. We must gather as much game as we can before the Cold Meal Moon is here. It will take us half of a days travel to reach the buffalo plains."

The warriors of the Ishak gathered quickly for the hunt. Fortier noticed that very few of them looked as bad as he felt. Once again, the excited chatter of the braves filled the camp. The warriors divided into small hunting parties of fifteen or sixteen braves, each setting out independently. Nementou and the warriors of the Vermilion Band were joined by five braves from a band of the Hikike that were familiar with the land they intended to hunt.

When Nementou's party reached the plain of buffalo, Fortier was astonished. The stretching prairie was covered with the beasts as far as the Frenchman could see. The braves concealed themselves in a stand of trees that bordered the plain and Fortier sat staring until he was joined by Nementou.

"Yok, my plan is to move the bowmen into that shallow ravine between here and the herd. Two men must move into the herd and drive some of the buffalo toward the ravine so our bowmen may shoot into them."

"What do you wish me to do?" Fortier asked.

"Are you feeling better now?"

"Yes, it seems the quick pace you set to this place has cleared my head."

"Good, then I would like you to take Escanimon and drive the buffalo to us."

"Nementou," Fortier said hesitantly, "I know that I have no skill with the bow, but I am not familiar with these beasts. I would not know how to force them to you in the ravine."

"You do not need knowledge, for as you said, they are beasts. Move very slowly into them and they will pay you no heed. When you are well into the herd, make sure that you are upwind of the ravine and then use your flint to set the prairie grass aflame. The fire and smoke will drive the buffalo to us."

Fortier and Escanimon sat patiently in the trees as the group of warriors crawled slowly to the ravine. When it was apparent that they were in position, the Frenchman and the young brave walked slowly toward the large herd. Fortier walked in a crouch until Escanimon noticed his stooped movement.

"Walk naturally, Yok. It is better to go slowly without any sudden moves that may alert the bulls. Follow my example, I have done this before."

When they moved among the beasts, Fortier felt a moment of panic when the strong musky odor of the animals assaulted his sense of smell. They seemed immense this close and the Frenchman tried to avert his gaze from the powerful bodies and sharp horns.

Fortier knew they were quite some distance from the ravine when Escanimon finally stopped and seated himself within an area with only a small scattering of buffalo. Fortier positioned himself twenty paces from the boy, yet still within the mostly vacant area. When he saw Escanimon striking his flint, he immediately did the same and was amazed at how quickly the tiny sparks ignited the dry prairie grass. He quickly cursed himself for not having tested the direction of the slight breeze, but was confident that Escanimon had remembered to do so.

As the fire spread, large billows of smoke rolled toward the nearby buffalo. The portion of the herd downwind of Fortier and the boy moved slowly at first, then thundered into a sprint as a large bull bellowed a warning from far to Fortier's left.

Fortier felt the plain vibrating for some moments after the buffalo had raced away. He glanced back at the majority of the herd still to his rear and was relieved to see them still placidly munching the prairie grass. Escanimon joined him and they wordlessly walked in the direction that the stampeded beasts had taken.

Some moments later they saw the first buffalo carcass. There were at least three arrows protruding from it and it was smoking from the fire that had raced over its body. There were only two more dead buffalo before the ravine.

As they reached the place of concealment for Nementou and his bowmen, they found eight more buffalo within the depression, being attended to by the hunters.

"A complete success," Katash yelled as he ran up to Fortier and Escanimon. "When we saw them coming we moved out of the ravine onto the far bank, away from the fire. We felled those three before they reached the ravine and then those eight fell into the old bayou. We finished them from the rim of the ravine very easily."

"If the other hunting parties have been this fortunate," Nementou said, joining them, "we may not hear the children cry from hunger when the Cold Meal Moon is upon us."

Fortier slipped down the side of the ravine brandishing his knife. As he busied himself skinning the first buffalo be reached, he heard Nementou call from above.

"Now you will have a fine, new robe, Yok; to warm you when the ice comes to the land of the Ishak.

# CHAPTER 14

*T*he Marquis de Gallo and his escort of ten dragoons topped the small hill and looked down on their destination. The mission appeared just as he had expected, desolate and remote. It was not much to look upon, but the Governor of the province of Texas knew well its importance to Spain.

The cursed French post of Natchitoches was rapidly becoming a bustling center for trade and something had to be done to block the French's rapid expansion westward. This mission had to be the Spanish obstacle. It was positioned in a good location, only nine leagues west of Natchitoches and away from the smothering thicket that surrounded the French post.

The Governor and his escort rode into the small outpost and were greeted by the commanding officer of the mission, Captain Bantera. The Governor knew Bantera had quite an impressive record of service. He had founded and once commanded the missions of San Francisco Xavier, Nuestra Senora de la Candelario and San Ildefonso, all on the San Gabriel River in central Texas. He had been assigned to San Miguel de los Adaes because of the mission's strategic importance, and he had thus far conducted the affairs of Spain in an exemplary fashion.

The Governor surveyed the small mission and realized that Bantera would soon require more resident troops. The mission at present was nothing more than ten cabins that housed Bantera, his twenty-five troops, two Franciscan friars and their housekeeper. A sizeable Indian village was in evidence just to the south of the mission, and the Marquis knew that Bantera would need more than twenty-five soldiers if insurrection ever evolved.

The Governor dismounted and shook hands warmly with Captain Bantera, although they had never met. The commanding officer was accompanied by one of the mission friars.

"Welcome to San Miguel de los Adaes, Marquis. I am Captain Joaquin de Orobio Bantera. May I also introduce the most Reverend Anthony Maragil, pastor of our mission."

The Governor was impressed by the dashing figure of Bantera. The priest, however, seemed frail and weak and the Governor's curt nod of greeting subtly demonstrated that the Marquis did not consider the church of utmost importance to his visit.

"Thank you, Captain Bantera. Unfortunately, my visit must be a brief one. If we may retire to your quarters, I would like to discuss our business immediately."

As the three men started for the mission's headquarters, the Governor stopped and addressed the mission pastor.

"Father Maragil, I would like to confer with Captain Bantera in private. You see, our business entails only military matters and I am sure you would find our conversation of no interest to yourself or the church."

"If your business concerns the mission," the priest stated quietly, "I am sure it would interest me, but I will concede to your judgment. Good day, Governor, I hope to see you again before you depart."

The Marquis and Captain Bantera entered the cabin and were offered refreshments by the commanding officer's steward. With brandy glasses in hand, the two Spaniards seated themselves in Bantera's office.

"Now," the Governor said, "your report on the mission."

"As you may have noticed, your Excellency, we have been able to move many of the local Caddos near the mission. They are becoming increasingly dependent on us for the trade goods we offer. Many of their men have given up hunting and their women have all but abandoned agriculture. We hire the men as hide hunters and mercenaries. They have taken to this change quickly and their women appreciate not having to tend fields."

"The ones that were hesitant to comply eventually were persuaded by goodly portions of tafia, the sugarcane rum that they openly clamor for. With the Caddos dependent on us, the French will not venture west of Natchitoches. They are having enough trouble controlling the Natchez, without having to contend with the Caddos as well."

"Excellent," the Marquis exclaimed. "All of this will go into my report. But now, on to my reason for visiting here. Tell me, Captain Bantera, have you had any trouble from the priest?"

"Well," the Captain answered carefully, "he does claim that we are making slaves of the Caddos. I explain to him that they are not in bondage; that they are compensated for their efforts, but he insists that I am making excuses. He has not been overly vocal because he himself has not had much success at converting them."

"You may have to prepare for more vehement protests from the Reverend Maragil", the Governor warned, "I have come to los Adaes to procure laborers to take with me west. We have many more missions to build and we need manpower. I need at least twenty healthy men and women and I intend to leave tomorrow."

"But how can I accomplish this, your Excellency?"

"It should not be difficult," the Governor intoned. "You simply invite the desired number to the mission tonight for a gathering in my honor, ply them with this tafia, and I take them west with me in the morning. Manacled, of course."

"There could be reprisals from the Caddos," the Captain warned.

"On my return to Texas, I will dispatch a force of fifty regulars to this mission. I am sure they will arrive before the Caddos can plan any rebellious activity."

"Have the reinforcements bring along many trade goods. That will appease the Caddos as much as any show of force."

"As you wish," the Governor placated.

"One more thing, your Excellency," Bantera said thoughtfully, "Do you foresee yourself returning in the future for more laborers?"

"That is very possible," the Governor answered. "Why do you ask?"

"Well," the Captain said as the plan quickly took shape in his mind, "there are many small tribes east and south of here that may be perfect pickings as laborers for the missions. I can hire Caddos to go and procure them, and not have to worry about reprisals. These tribes numbers are few, and any retaliation they mount could be dealt with easily."

"Brilliant, Captain Bantera," the Governor exclaimed, "You are truly a hero to Spain."

"Thank you, your Excellency," the Captain answered, beaming. "Now shall we plan this evenings festivities?"

The two Spaniards laughed heartily and poured more brandy.

Kata's son was born on the fourth day of the Walnut Noon. Fortier was happy that the birth took place as the first signs of spring became apparent for the Cold Meal Moon had been an ordeal.

With the New Year had come howling winds from the north accompanied by incessant rains. The horde of buffalo meat and venison that had been stockpiled during the brief hunting period had been consumed quickly. The Frenchman had attempted to persuade Nementou and the other Chief's to implement some form of rationing system, but had met with indifference to his pleas. The Chief's had simply waved him off and accepted the diminishing supply of

food as stoically as they accepted the freezing temperatures and tor-
rential rains.

By the time of the Chestnut Moon the meat was gone and the
people subsisted on meager portions of dried corn and broths con-
cocted from the small animals the warriors were fortunate enough to
occasionally trap. Fortier found it extremely difficult to follow the
practice of the people when the rains fell for long periods. They
would all stay indoors for as many as three days at a time, going
without any solid nourishment of any kind and drinking only water.
Their peculiar habit of filling their stomachs with water and effort-
lessly throwing it up was one he could never understand or participate in. Everyone seemed convinced that this was an especially
healthy practice and Fortier could find no argument to discredit
their belief.

Although he still had no contact with Kata, he had occupied the
days monitoring her progress toward motherhood. From the time of
their arrival at the winter camp, she had been isolated in a specially
built hut where she was attended to by Yuk' hiti and a number of
other older women from other bands.

When the Frenchman received word of the child's birth, his quick
calculation made him realize that Kata had been carrying the child
when they had made the journey to Cata-Oula. He could not help
but wonder if she or Soco had been aware of this. He decided to erase
this fact from his mind rather than have another unknown aspect of
the strange last few months plague his thoughts.

For the first weeks after the birth of the child, Fortier had enjoyed
watching Kata and the infant when they left the birthing hut and
moved back to the hut of Yuk' hiti. From his own hut, the Frenchman studied the two busy women as they would strap the sturdy boy
to a piece of bark, bent to fit the child's body, and move about the
encampment with their duties.

Seated near the entrance to his hovel, Fortier waved as he noticed
Nementou emerge from his own hut on a chilly but sunny morning.

The Frenchman felt his stomach grumble but this did not dissuade his bright mood, brought about by the recent bird migrations north, a sure sign that winter had indeed ended.

Nementou started toward Fortier's hut, stopped abruptly, and reversed direction. The Frenchman stared curiously at the retreating form of the Chief when he noticed Nementou look back with an amused smile. Fortier started to rise to follow the smiling Nementou when he sensed a presence to his rear. He turned to find Kata, holding her child, standing two paces away.

The startled Frenchman surged to his feet quickly, completely at a loss for words. He stared at the woman and her infant for long moments, feeling foolish and insecure in her presence.

"Hello Hiyen," Kata said, smiling. "I would like for you to meet Tortue."

"Tortue," Fortier whispered when he found his tongue. "It is a fine name. He is such a good-looking boy, Kata. I have been watching you and I am so happy that the boy fares well."

"It seems strange," Kata said shyly, "to be speaking Ishak with you. It is good…to be speaking with you."

"Oh Kata," Fortier breathed, advancing a step and then checking himself, "I have missed you."

"I have missed you as well, Hiyen. You fought bravely against the Tunica. Has your wound healed well?"

"It was nothing," an embarrassed Fortier answered, "I was fortunate in that fight; everything happened so quickly."

A sudden squeal from the child brought a surprised chuckle from the Frenchman. Kata smiled and kneeling, rapidly replaced the soiled moss between the infant's legs with a fresh wad of the plant she took from within her robe.

"He will be a mighty chief someday with that voice," Fortier laughed.

Completing her task, Kata looked up, her face etched in sadness. Fortier knelt before her, once again at a loss for words.

"Hiyen, I have love for you. I know from everything that you do that you want me for your woman. Yuk' hiti advises that soon she will go to the place above and that Tortue and I will need someone to care for us. She says I should come to you now."

Fortier sat speechless. He had prayed to hear these words from Kata, and now that she had uttered them, he sat staring dumbly, unable to too easily accept what he had thought he might never hear. As he spoke what was in his heart, he still felt the omnipresent twinge of guilt.

"I do love you, Kata. I yearn to have you and Tortue share my hut. I would care for him as I would you. I…"

"Please Hiyen," Kata interrupted, crying quietly. "Please understand that it would be so easy for me to come to you. But I fear what is still always in my head. I will never forget Chaoui. I so fear that he would always be between us and you may grow to resent that. I am so unsure…"

"Kata," Fortier spoke, grasping Kata's shoulders firmly. "Do not torture yourself this way. I have learned from Nementou that grief cannot go on forever. It almost destroyed him, but he has learned to deal with it and it has made him a better man. We must learn from this. I will never forget Chaoui either. I owe him my life."

Fortier rose and paced for a moment collecting his thoughts. Kata sat silently staring at the infant cradled in her arms.

"I am Ishak now," Fortier said, as he ceased his pacing. "I am Yok of the Vermilion Band and I am proud that I have earned warrior status. I want you to stop listening to the dire warnings of Yuk' hiti. You and Tortue will always be cared for, whether it is as my woman or not. You need not hurry into deciding what you truly feel. If it is right, in time you will come to me. Not because some old birthing woman advises you on security, but because you want to be with me. I will be here when you are ready. And if you are never ready, I will still be here."

They sat conversing quietly for most of the day. Nementou had stationed himself outside of his own hut and discreetly intercepted and turned away a few curious villagers that had planned to visit Yok when Kata was seen sitting there.

Late in the afternoon Kata and the infant Tortue returned to the hut of Yuk' hiti and Fortier joined Nementou. The Chief remained quiet until the Frenchman broke the silence.

"Thank you for keeping the curious away from my hut," Fortier mumbled.

Nementou merely nodded, staring across the river.

"You heard most of our conversation?" Fortier inquired.

"Yes, I did," Nementou replied, turning to the Frenchman.

"And what do you think?" Fortier asked shyly.

"I think," Nementou said, smiling, "that now you are truly Ishak."

# CHAPTER 15

※

*T*he winter camp of the Ishak was beginning to break. The Calcasieu Band of the Hiye Kiti had departed for their spring and summer home two days earlier. The band from the Hikike had left a few hours past, and could still just be seen, moving slowly west, far across the river.

The Vermilion and Teche Bands had begun preparations to travel that morning and expected to leave in one more day's time. Some of the women had gone into the forest to gather some of the fresh new sprouts for meals on the journey, and the men were packing their bundles for loading on lodgepoles.

Skunnemoke was examining Fortier's puckered arrow wound for one last time and clucking about the foolishness of young men and their battles. When the old shaman was done, the Frenchman walked to Nementou's hut and joined the Chief and Katash.

"Why don't we leave at first light?" Katash was asking the chief. "My mouth waters when I think of the clams I will eat."

"Katash could build his own midden with the clams he eats," Fortier said laughing.

"Yok is full of jokes," Katash said, elbowing Nementou's side, "now that he spends so much time with Kata."

Fortier looked to Nementou and the Chief's serious countenance broke with a vivid smile.

"I cannot dispute his words, Yok," Nementou laughed.

Fortier grunted and playfully wrestled Katash to the ground. Katash's giggles and Nementou's laughter were cut short by a piercing scream from far in the forest. The men hurriedly gathered to Nementou with weapons in hand. As they moved toward the trees, two of the plant gathering women ran into the encampment.

"Caddos," one of the shrieking women wailed. "They tried to take us."

"Who is still in the forest?" Nementou yelled.

"Yuk' hiti fought them," the woman said, composing herself. "We escaped because Yuk' hiti fought them with her knife. They have killed her."

"Where is Kata?" Fortier screamed. "Tell me woman, have they harmed Kata or Tortue?"

"It is so terrible," the woman cried, "they have taken Kata and the boy."

Fortier dashed toward the trees but was stopped by Nementou's sharp command.

"Yok, you must wait!"

Fortier ran back to the assembled villagers.

"Nementou," he pleaded, "they have taken Kata and Tortue!"

"If we follow too near, they will kill them to travel faster and avoid being overtaken. We must plan this if we wish to retrieve them alive."

Nementou turned to the woman and spoke calmly, "How many Caddos did you see?"

"Four or maybe five," the woman whimpered.

The Chief looked to the forest and was lost in thought for a time. Fortier paced furiously, not able to contain his fierce anxiety.

"This will take some time, and it must be done right," the Chief announced. "We cannot delay our departure to our summer camp for as long as it may take to find Kata and Tortue. Katash, you are to lead the Vermilion Band until I return. Take our people to the summer camp and guide them wisely. Yok and I will follow the Caddos and free Kata and the boy. We will join the village at our summer camp when we have succeeded."

It took Nementou a while to put down the flurry of protests that erupted after his announcement. When order ensued, Katash addressed Nementou calmly.

"Let me accompany Yok. I can track these Caddos better than either of you and you can certainly guide the people better than I.

"Please understand," Nementou said patiently, "for the safety of our band, we cannot send more than two warriors after Kata and Tortue. Also understand that I must be one of the two that go for this is Chaoui's son. I must go after my brother's son."

The assembled villagers dispersed quickly as Fortier and Nementou prepared for their mission. The Frenchman gathered his weapons and was handed a hurriedly packed pouch of food by Patassa. He stood patiently waiting as the Chief spoke quietly to his woman, embraced her warmly and turned to depart. The two Ishak warriors sprinted wordlessly into the forest.

Fortier and Nementou had little trouble following the kidnappers. When they had overtaken the party of Caddos, they observed from concealment that the village woman may have only seen four or five Caddos, but there were indeed eight in the party. It had been difficult for Nementou to restrain Fortier from charging into the group when they had seen Kata and the child being herded through the forest with two other captives that appeared to be Avoyels. They had remained at least half a kilometer back from the Caddos lest they detect pursuit.

When they reached the river of red clay, they found that the Caddos had embarked in pirogues that had been waiting concealed along the shore. It was obvious that the kidnappers were undoubtedly headed for the post of Natchitoches. Neither Fortier nor Nementou had ever been to the French post, but they were both aware of where it was located. They hurriedly decided to strike for the post overland, rather than take the time to construct a pirogue for themselves.

After two days of fighting their way slowly through the tangled undergrowth and avoiding encounters with the many wild animals that seemed to inhabit the thicket, they regretted their decision not to take the time to construct a watercraft. They were driven on by the knowledge that the Caddos were steadily increasing the gap between themselves and their pursuers.

On the morning of the fifth day since Kata and Tortue's capture, Fortier and Nementou emerged from the immense thicket onto a level plain. The post of Natchitoches could he seen in the distance and the two men broke into a lope, in spite of their weary condition.

As they approached the main gate of the garrison, Fortier could hear the conversation of two French soldiers stationed in one of the stockade's four blockhouses positioned on the corners of the walled town.

"Those two do not look familiar," the soldier apparently on duty said to the officer standing at his side.

"If they are Natchez, shoot them," the officer answered.

"We are not Natchez," Fortier called to the two soldiers in his native language, "We are Ishak and we would like permission to enter your garrison."

The two soldiers stared in amazement at the two braves standing below their watchtower.

"What tribe is Ishak?" the officer called, finally finding his tongue.

"You know us as Atakapa," Fortier answered. "We would like to speak to your commanding officer."

"How does an Atakapa come to speak the French language so well?" the soldier on duty inquired.

"I was French before I became Ishak. My name is Gabriel Fortier and I seek information from your commanding officer."

As the pair were admitted entrance to the post, Fortier quickly surveyed the area, looking for signs of captives. The town consisted of seven large buildings, situated immediately inside the log walls of the garrison, surrounding an impressive looking center building that was apparently the post headquarters. A long barracks to the rear of the post housed what had to be over a hundred troops, the Frenchman surmised. The trading post was located just inside the main gate and a quite respectable appearing chapel stood to the left of the large trading center that occupied two of the buildings.

The officer from the wall approached Fortier and Nementou with a smile, tempered by his hand that rested on the hilt of his sword.

"Welcome to Fort St. Jean Baptiste des Natchitoches," the officer said. "I am Lieutenant Francois Blondel de La Tour, second in command here."

"Thank you, Lieutenant. We would like to have a moment of your commanding officer's time. We are seeking my companion's sister-in-law and her child. They were abducted by a raiding party of Caddos and we suspect that they have come here."

"If they were Caddos," the Lieutenant answered, "they did not come here. Come, I think our commander may wish to hear your story. He is very busy because of the Natchez problem we are experiencing, but I think he will find time to speak to you."

The trio entered the center building. Fortier could not help but notice Nementou's curious gaze as he studied the interior of the large building. No doubt he had never been inside of a white man's dwelling.

The Lieutenant had been gone for only a short time when he returned accompanied by the imposing figure of a man Fortier guessed to be in his fifties; silver headed and barrel-chested. He was bedecked in the finery of a French Commander and he strode directly to Fortier and extended his hand.

"Good day, I am Commander Louis Chevernet of the army of France. Lieutenant de La Tour informs me that you have had some problem with the Caddos?"

"Yes Sir," Fortier answered. "My companions sister-in-law and her child were abducted by a party of Caddos and we followed them to the river of red clay. They proceeded west on the river in pirogues and we surmised that they were coming here."

"Where were they taken from you?"

"Many leagues south of here on a river my people call the Calcasieu. Following them, we noticed that there were other captives besides the woman and child we seek. We believe them to have been Avoyels."

The two French officers stared at one another for a moment and then the Lieutenant spoke.

"The Spanish are up to something. I am sure they have put the Caddos up to this."

"We cannot concern ourselves with this now, Lieutenant," the Commander answered, "The Natchez are approaching and that situation must be dealt with."

"What is going on here?" Fortier interrupted.

"Let us adjourn to my office and I will explain," Chevernet said patiently.

When the four men were seated in the commander's spartan office, he addressed Fortier.

"The Spanish government has built and occupied a mission west of here. It is a religious mission and yet they are using it to restrict our movement westward. They do not want French settlers in their Texas lands. They have repressed and coerced the Caddo tribe to the point that they have become the tools of the Spanish. I fear from what you have said, that they are now having the Caddos abduct people for some Spanish scheme I cannot guess at this time. One guess I can make is that the woman and child you seek are at the mission of los Adaes, nine leagues west of here."

"Can you afford us any assistance in the rescue of our people?" Fortier asked.

"I am truly sorry," Chevernet said with sympathy. "I cannot risk trouble with Spain at this time. We are facing the potential of war as it is, here in Natchitoches. You see, the Natchez tribe has never accepted our presence here. We have become allies with the Tunica and Avoyels, but the Natchez stubbornly oppose our occupying this land. I have received word that a force of some six hundred Natchez warriors intend to assault Natchitoches and that, I assure you, is my highest priority right now."

"What is your garrison strength?" Fortier queried.

"One hundred fifty regulars, sixty male civilians and one hundred Avoyel and Tunica volunteers," the Lieutenant answered.

"Do not give that information out too quickly, Lieutenant," Chevernet admonished.

"Don't worry, Commander," Fortier said, "we do not spy for the Natchez. I wish we could stay and assist you in your defense, but we must be off for this Spanish mission."

"Good luck to you, Fortier," de La Tour said emotionally. "I wish there was time for you to tell me your story of how you came to be an Atakapa."

As the men stood, there was a loud rap on the office door. Chevernet called admittance and a breathless soldier burst into the room.

"Commander," he said excitedly, "the Natchez have arrived. It appears the post is surrounded. We are under siege."

Kata was afraid. When she and Tortue had first been taken she had told herself that somehow Hiyen would find a way to rescue them. After all, hadn't he found a way to avenge Chaoui? She had not let the fear overcome her for at least three days. The Caddos had treated all of the captives well. They had done nothing to instigate fear amongst the prisoners.

When they had arrived at this white man's town, she had begun to have doubts. She knew that if Hiyen was following, he should have had no trouble keeping up with their slow pace. So where was he?

The prisoners had been herded into a large wooden hut by a group of strange white men that looked like Cannouche but were different. Kata did not understand their language as she did the Cannouche. When she had tried to communicate with them in Hiyen's French they had sneered and ignored her. Now she and Tortue sat on the floor of this wooden hut with ten other captives awaiting they knew not what. None of the other prisoners in the room were Ishak and Kata felt foreign and alone. Fortunately, Tortue was a strong and healthy baby and he did not seem affected by the ordeal thusfar.

The door of the wooden lodge was opened by one of the white warriors that had driven the captives into the hut and a strange looking white man entered. He wore black robes that reached to the ground. The captives were much impressed by the gleaming cross of shiny flint that hung on his chest. He moved to the center of the lodge and spoke in the strange language of the white captors. He was met by silence and he started from the lodge shaking his head. He stopped and spoke again, this time in the French language of the Cannouche.

"If none of you understands Spanish, I suppose none of you understand French either?"

Glancing around, Kata realized that none of the other captives understood what the white man had said. She was afraid to answer and once again the man started for the door. Impulsively she stood and addressed the black-robed man.

"Will you tell us why we are being held here?"

The white man stopped abruptly and turned, seeking whom had spoken. Seeing Kata, he advanced on her with a look of kindness on his face.

"You speak French; what tribe are you?"

"I am of the Ishak. Please, why have we been taken? I fear for my child."

The priest seemed to notice Tortue for the first time and a look of disgust flashed across his features.

"The barbarians," he said to himself in Spanish, "they even stoop to kidnapping infants."

"I do not understand," Kata said.

"Forgive me, my child. My name is Father Maragil. I want you to know that I will ensure that all of you are fed well and not mistreated. You must urge these others not to attempt escape, for the soldiers have orders to shoot anyone that does. You will not he here long, but while you are, I promise that no harm will come to you."

"What is this place and if we are not to be here long, where are we being taken?" Kata pleaded.

"This is the mission of San Miguel de Los Adaes and the best I can discern is that you are to be taken to some destination in the lands of Texas," Maragil said sympathetically.

"Where is this lands of Texas?"

"Many leagues west of here. Tell me my dear, where is your husband?"

"He has gone to the place above," Kata answered.

"I see, well, you and your child will adapt to the rolling hills of Texas. Your life there will probably be better than what you have known in your own land."

"But why are we being taken there?" Kata asked in confusion.

"To build more missions like this one. Spain is colonizing and needs native laborers. It will not be a bad life once you have adjusted."

"When will we be allowed to return to our people?" Kata called after the priest as he walked to the door.

The priest stopped at the entrance, looked back at Kata and shook his head sadly. Tapping on the door he exited rapidly when it was opened. Kata returned to her seat and hugged Tortue fiercely. Hurry Hiyen, hurry, she prayed silently.

# CHAPTER 16

*I*t was the third day of the siege of the garrison of Natchitoches. The large Natchez force had indeed surrounded the post and Chevernet had remained inside the stout walls, waiting to find out what the Natchez would do. The post was well provisioned and the commander hoped to avoid a fight if the Natchez warriors became bored with waiting. They had chosen not to storm the garrison and had positioned themselves out of the range of fire from the walls, yelling taunts and insults.

Fortier and Nementou had cursed the timing of the siege for they were confined to the post until the Natchez departed or were driven off. They had thought of trying to slip out of the post and attempt to elude the Natchez but Chevernet had forbid it. He maintained that they would not get past the open plain to the forest and capture meant certain death.

They had slept outside of the trading center, although Lieutenant de La Tour had offered them accommodations in the barracks. Nementou had declined the offer to sleep inside of the wooden lodge.

When Fortier awoke on the third day, he was surprised to find Nementou still wrapped in his robe, unmoving. He rose to find the Chief sweating profusely and moaning with discomfort. Nementou told him that he had been forced to rush to the rear of the trading buildings all night long to squat and relieve himself of the sickness that seemed to explode from his bowels. He complained of severe muscular aches and Fortier realized he was infected with high fever. The Frenchman's urging to take Nementou to the post doctor was refused. The Chief insisted he would feel better soon, and if he did not, he would visit Skunnemoke upon their return to Ishak lands.

The Frenchman had left the Chief wrapped in his robe, eaten the breakfast offered to him by the Lieutenant, and now wandered around the post for a better look at the town. He stood admiring the handsome chapel located in the northeast corner of the garrison when he was joined by a young friar.

"Good morning young man," the priest said softly. "I understand you are the French civilian that lives with the Indian band."

Fortier turned to the priest and realized he was young but not as young as he first thought. His face bore the pockmarks of disease and he seemed frail.

"Yes, I choose to live with the Ishak."

"And what are you called?"

"Yok, Hiyen. You may call me Gabriel."

"I am pleased to know you Gabriel. I am Father Poirier."

"I have never known a priest," Fortier said, turning back to the church.

"Perhaps you have never needed to know one?"

"Why would one need to know a priest?"

"For many different reasons, "Poirier answered. "May I ask you a question?"

"Of course."

"Why do you choose to live with these Ishak?"

Fortier pondered the question for a moment before answering.

"I suppose I never knew responsibility until I came to be with these people. This responsibility has given me purpose and I suppose that has given me happiness and that is enough for me to choose to stay with them."

"And how far does this responsibility go?"

"I am not sure I know what you mean."

"Are you not aware of what is happening to these people?"

"You mean the settlers moving in?" Fortier asked nonchalantly.

"Come inside and sit with me," the priest said, "I would like to be sure that you are aware of the depth of this responsibility you say you have."

They entered the vestry and seated themselves. Fortier's curiosity was piqued by the grave tone of the priest from the moment he launched into his speech.

He spoke of the innocence of the majority of these natives, how they had much more to fear than simply being driven from their ancestral homes by the settlers. He informed Fortier of how measles, smallpox, cholera and even influenza were inflicting terrible tolls on the native population. He spoke of dishonest traders plying the tribes with alcohol to gain their dependency.

The priest spoke long about the power struggle being waged between France and Spain and how the local tribes were already being caught in the middle of this.

"If you really have a responsibility to these people, help them. Don't just use them for whatever it is they have given you or done for you, but help them. It will not be an easy task but if you truly mean what you said of them earlier, you will be up to it."

Fortier left the sacristy and returned to the trading post. Nementou was still wrapped in his robe and did not look well, so the Frenchman proceeded to try to locate the post doctor.

Shouts from the east wall of the garrison beckoned the post commander and Fortier decided to investigate. He scaled the ladder to the large blockhouse to find it occupied by de La Tour and several soldiers. The Lieutenant greeted Fortier and pointed out over the wall to the clearing.

A large group of Natchez could be seen leading a figure to a stake embedded in the ground. The warriors were in a frenzy and Fortier felt the hair at the nape of his neck tingle. The figure they led was a white woman that they proceeded to tie to the stake. Dry brush was stacked at the feet of the woman and Fortier could hear her high-pitched screams over the guttural whoops of the Natchez.

Chevernet entered the blockhouse and walked to the wall.

"It is a French woman, Commander," de La Tour said sourly. "They must have taken her from some homestead."

"I can see what is happening," Chevernet spat.

The Natchez began dancing and yelling when the dry brush crackled into flames. The fire quickly licked at the billowing skirt of the woman and as she was engulfed, her screams became inhuman. One of the soldiers in the blockhouse leaned over the parapet and vomited violently.

"They are doing this to draw us out," de La Tour mumbled.

"They have succeeded," Chevernet barked. "Lieutenant, assemble the garrison. I want every troop, every male civilian and our Avoyel and Tunica allies ready to advance on the Natchez in fifteen minutes. We will drive directly into them and make them pay for this atrocity."

When the main gate of the post opened, the Natchez had fallen back from the smoldering corpse of the French woman. Chevernet led the force out of the post at quick march, holding his sword before him. The trained regulars of the French army bore into the Natchez warriors with muskets blazing and bayonets poised. The screaming warriors broke ranks quickly and turned in full retreat.

When Fortier saw this, still standing in the blockhouse, he rushed to Nementou's side. The Chief raised himself from his prone position when Fortier told him of the recent events. He staggered to his feet and grasped the side of the building for support.

"Stay here, Nementou," Fortier urged. "I will go and get Kata and Tortue."

"I will go with you, Yok," Nementou said weakly.

"You must stay here. You are too ill to come with me."

"You are a war chief, Yok," Nementou whispered, "but I am Chief of the Vermilion Band and I say I will go with you."

"As you wish," Fortier relented. "Let us go quickly while the Natchez are gone."

As they started west, Fortier prayed silently. "Hold on, Kata. I am coming. Just hold on."

Fortier lay concealed in a thick stand of trees observing the Spanish mission of los Adaes. Finding the mission had not been difficult but it had taken the Frenchman much longer than he had anticipated to reach because of their slow travel.

Nementou's condition was not good and it was obvious that the Chief was dangerously weak. Even now he lay within a small thicket jerking with chills from the fever that raged in him.

A fine mist of rain dripped through the trees from the low ceiling of dark gray clouds that hung overhead. Crawling silently back to Nementou's position, Fortier shook the chief from his semi-conscious state gently.

"I think I know where the captives are being held. I can see guards outside of a cabin and two baskets of what I think was food was just brought to that cabin."

"Yok," Nementou muttered weakly, "wait for nightfall. Then go and get Kata and the boy. When you have freed them, go as quickly as you can to the French post. You will be safe there."

"Wait for us here, Nementou. We will all make it to Natchitoches."

"Yok, do as I say. When darkness comes, I will use the last of my strength to draw the attention of the white men. You must use this opportunity to rescue Kata and Tortue. Do not wait for me. It is the only chance they have, Yok. If you truly wish to save them, you must do as I say."

Fortier shook his head in exasperation. He knew what Nementou said was true. With the pathetically slow pace of the Chief they would never avoid capture; even it he managed to release Kata and Tortue. Damn these Spanish slavers, he thought.

"Yok, make Kata your woman. Do not wait for her to decide. Her mind is still clouded by grief and guilt and she needs you to help her deal with this. Take care of them, Yok. And be sure Tortue knows of his father. Please, tell him often of Chaoui."

Before Fortier could answer, Nementou fell back against the ground into prostration with shallow, ragged breaths. He seemed barely conscious so the Frenchman remained silent. He sat waiting for nightfall, knowing that he would have to affect the rescue of Kata and the boy alone.

Darkness came quickly because of the inclement weather. Nementou summoned the strength that remained in him and rose from his prone position. His head swam with dizziness as he emerged from the thicket followed by Yok. He did not know how long his strength would last so he spoke quickly,

"Try to get as near to the lodge that holds Kata and the boy as you can without being detected. When the time is right, overcome the guards, take Kata and Tortue and flee. Remember that their lives will depend on how quickly you act."

"What do you plan?" Yok asked. "How will I know the time is right to go for them?"

"I am not sure right now," Nementou answered in a breathy whisper. "Wait until something happens that you feel sure is my doing."

"Nementou, there must be some other way."

"Silence!" the Chief countered. "There is no other way."

Nementou relaxed his stern manner and grasped the shoulders of Yok affectionately.

"My brother, I am doing what I choose to do. Remember you once told me you spoke with old Yok of how we choose our paths in life? I am choosing mine now. I am not familiar with this sickness that is upon me but I know that it will send me above before I can reach

Skunnemoke or any of our shamans. All I ask is that you tell our people...tell Patassa..."

The Chief shook with a violent tremor that prevented him from continuing. He held onto the Frenchman until the shivering subsided and then he started for the mission.

When Nementou had moved some distance from Fortier he stopped and looked back at the Frenchman. He smiled and signed, "Remember me."

Nementou moved slowly to the opposite side of the mission from where he knew Yok was destined. He was forced to stop periodically and clutch his stomach to prevent himself from gasping at the sharp pain that emanated from his bowels. His vision was blurred but he managed to work his way to the tall, pointed wooden lodge situated at the end of the row of wood huts. Peering into the darkness past the tall lodge, he could detect cookfires from what appeared to be a village some distance from the mission. The mission was quiet but he could hear voices coming from some of the occupied huts.

The tall lodge was dark and still when he moved to the entrance. This suited his purpose well. He studied the latch on the entrance for a moment, released it and entered the lodge in one motion. He scanned the dark interior for a moment and satisfied himself that he was alone. He moved slowly past the long rows of seats to what appeared to be a ritual bench situated before the seating area. His plan formulated the moment he saw the thin white skins draped over the ritual bench. He gathered them into a bundle and placed them under the bench and began striking his flint, struggling with his weakness. The skins ignited quickly from the shower of sparks and Nementou moved to the entrance.

Before he could quit the lodge, the entrance opened and a white man in long black skins entered. He smiled at Nementou and then looked past the Chief and noticed the flames. His pleasant face suddenly registered horror and he screamed words Nementou did not understand. As the white man turned for the entrance shouting obvious words of warning, Nementou swung his war club, shattering the man's head. He dropped with a thud and remained silent.

Moving to the entrance, the Chief heard a chorus of shouts from outside the lodge and, stealing a glance out of the opening, saw white men with firesticks converging on the tall lodge. He looked back to the ritual bench and was satisfied to see the flames licking up the walls to the top of the lodge.

Nementou moved back into the lodge as far as he could without being burned and wearily strung his bow. A white man charged into the lodge shouting and was quickly silenced by an arrow from the Chief. Nementou peered with fading vision at the opening and saw white men pouring into the lodge. The second man through the entrance stumbled and fell over the body of the man in black skins and Nementou chuckled as he drove an arrow into him. He felt the flames teasing his back when a host of muskets flashed from the entrance of the lodge. The Chief spun from the impact and crashed into the burning altar and as it toppled, a shower of sparks ignited new flames throughout the already burning chapel.

Fortier was crouched behind a barrel not more than ten paces from the guards stationed outside of the cabin being used as a prison. He had begun to wonder if maybe he should make his attempt without waiting for Nementou. In his weakened condition, the Chief may be lying unconscious somewhere inside the mission.

A shout from the far end of the compound attracted the attention of the guards and Fortier prepared to spring for the cabin entrance. The guards conversed excitedly and one of them sprinted away in the direction of the shout.

Fortier saw a number of soldiers rush out of the nearby cabins clutching muskets and buckets. The Frenchman dashed for the remaining guard brandishing his knife and crashing into the unsuspecting soldier, drove the weapon deep into his chest. The guard muttered a surprised grunt and crumpled to the ground.

Crashing into the cabin, Fortier surveyed the dark interior and sensed the presence of a number of people.

"Kata," he hissed sharply. "Kata, if you are here, come to me."

The girl, holding her child, rushed to the Frenchman as an eerie glow of light filtered into the open door of the cabin. Fortier could see men and women scattered throughout the cabin and looking back to the door, saw tall flames begin to light the night sky. Kata hugged him fiercely and they both shuddered when the crash of musket fire rang through the mission.

Fortier rushed from the cabin tugging Kata as Tortue began to wail from the jouncing. Looking back, Fortier saw the other captives quickly pouring from the cabin and running into many different directions.

When they reached the edge of the forest they stopped and Fortier could clearly see the mission chapel totally engulfed in flames. Kata hurriedly managed to pacify Tortue and his cries suddenly became whimpers.

Fortier took one last look at the burning church.

"Good-bye, my brother," he whispered. "You will not be forgotten."

Fortier took the baby from Kata and they sprinted away from the mission without any further hesitation.

# CHAPTER 17

✿

*F*ortier and Kata moved happily through the scented forest heading south. The baby Tortue dozed contentedly on his bark cradleboard strapped securely to Fortier's back. They expected to reach the lands of the Vermilion Band today and they were in a joyous frame of mind.

The past three weeks had been spent at the post of Natchitoches. Their flight from los Adaes had been tedious and trying but they had eluded the pursuit of the Spanish, if there had been any. On one occasion during the escape east they had heard the sounds of musket fire far behind them, and this had driven them on faster.

They had arrived at Natchitoches to find that the French had won a decisive victory over the Natchez. Chevernet's attack had killed over sixty Natchez warriors and sent the remainder scurrying north and away from the French post. The French casualties had been nominal and Chevernet was confident that the Natchez problem was resolved for the time being.

Their stay in Natchitoches had at first been awkward for Kata. It had been days before she could be made to understand that the French could be trusted. The uniforms of the soldiers of the post of Natchitoches did not differ from the Spanish uniforms very much in her eyes.

Fortier had spent hours trying to explain to her the peculiarities of the Spanish after she had related to him her conversation with the mission priest, Father Maragil. He struggled to make her see the differences between the French and the Spanish to no avail. The post of Natchitoches was far too similar to los Adaes in Kata's eyes.

They also had to deal with the loss of Nementou. They had conversed long about the Chief. His weaknesses, his strengths, and the journey he had taken to becoming a great leader to his people. The Ishak did not mourn the passing of the dead, but Fortier and Kata mourned the loss of Nementou. He had become so close to them after Chaoui's death that they knew he and his wisdom would be sorely missed.

Fortier and the Reverend Poirier spent much time together after Kata adjusted to the post. Fortier found the young priest much wiser than his years and when he thought of how much he was learning from the Jesuit he realized that perhaps a person could need a priest. He also realized that they were becoming very good friends.

After two weeks at the post, Father Poirier married Fortier and Kata in the chapel of St. Jean Baptiste. Lieutenant de La Tour stood in attendance to Fortier and the Avoyel housekeeper of Commander Chevernet stood with Kata. It was a fine ceremony attended by much of the garrison and there was much celebration after the service.

As the newlywed couple and their child followed the winding vermilion-stained bayou on which they knew they would find their band, they spoke soft words of endearment to one another. They spoke of wishing to find peace in the land of the Ishak and ensure a safe and happy environment for Tortue to grow in. Nearing the site of the summer village, Fortier addressed his wife quizzically.

"Kata, I cannot understand why you see so little difference between the Spanish and the French."

Walking along, Kata turned to her husband with an amused glint in her eye. She knew he enjoyed bantering with her and their topics of conversation often tested each other's minds.

"It seems," Kata began, "that all white men practice the same curious customs is all I have said. Our Chitimacha neighbors to the east live in permanent homes; we Ishak live in movable lodges. The Natchez build temples for worship similar to the white man's churches; we build no such temples but worship outside of our lodges. I saw very little difference between the slavers mission and the post of Natchitoches."

"Well, at least the French are not making slaves of the tribes," Fortier said self-righteously.

"Are you so sure, Hiyen? The Avoyels and Tunicas at the post seemed to jump at the white chief's bidding. Chevernet's housekeeper told me that many from her tribe would sell their children to get some of the white man's goods. In a way, that can be called slavery."

"You sound like Father Poirier," Fortier answered.

The couple accelerated their pace when they passed the evidence of a recent village site. They knew that the band had probably moved farther south to be closer to the great water and the anticipation gave the travelers energy.

"You can't deny that many of the white man's goods are very useful," Fortier continued.

"And many of them," Kata retorted, "are foolish."

"What do you mean?"

"For example, these windows the white men put in their lodges. They say they put them in to let the sunshine into the lodge. Then they cover them with skins. It seems to me that only the entrance is necessary, that can be used to let the sunshine in and as an entrance."

Fortier shook his head and after a moment laughed at his wife's reasoning.

It was a happy and yet melancholy homecoming when they reached the village. The happiness on all the familiar faces seeing Fortier, Kata and the new band member Tortue turned to sadness when the travelers related the fate of Nementou. Fortier and Kata told of the entire experience, including their marriage, before the assembly broke up. There were sighs and nods of approval from everyone when the couple told of their joining.

It was near dark and the weather was mild so Fortier and Kata quickly constructed a lean-to hut that would prove adequate until a proper hut could be built. A breeze sifted through the moss-laden trees and Fortier smiled contentedly as he sat outside of the newly constructed lean-to. Kata emerged from the makeshift hut and spoke quietly.

"Tortue is asleep. I must go and comfort Patassa. If Tortue awakens, please come for me."

"Don't worry, Kata. I can look after the boy."

Kata smiled; caressed Fortier's face and then walked across the encampment. Fortier sat listening to the hum of the cicadas and breathing the perfume of the blooming magnolias. He turned and saw Katash approaching warily.

"Are you sleeping, Yok?"

"No, please join me. I was just enjoying the evening."

The two men sat quietly for some time. The silence was comfortable but Fortier sensed an anxiety in Katash.

"We will surely miss Nementou," Fortier said, breaking the stillness.

Katash leaned forward and seemed to take Fortier's comment as his cue to speak.

"Yok, I am troubled. I have done Nementou's bidding and led the band here. Everyone says I have done well but I have not been called on for any decisions. I am a tracker and hunter, Yok. I am no chief and I do not want to be a chief. This responsibility keeps me from sleeping and I cannot continue at this any longer."

"Perhaps someone else should be chosen as chief, if you feel this strongly about this, Katash."

"I have spoken to every warrior since your return," Katash proclaimed excitedly, "and there are more of us now since the Cold Meal

Moon gathering. Six braves and four women have joined us from other bands. I have spoken to everyone and we all agree that you should be Chief."

Fortier sprang to his feet and exclaimed loudly.

"What?" You cannot mean this. I am a Cannouche, how can I lead a band of the Ishak?"

"You were once a Cannouche," Katash corrected. "Now you are Father of Tortue, Hiye Kiti Ishak and a war chief at that. You may be chosen Chief of the band."

"My head is swimming," Fortier confessed. "Please, allow me some time to myself. We will speak of this in the morning."

"As you wish," Katash said, and then quickly crossed the camp center back to his own hut.

Fortier seated himself and thought of this strange turn of events. He began planning a refusal the villagers would accept when the words of Father Poirier reached out from the corner of his mind.

*"What is your responsibility to these people?"* he had asked. The long list of disease fatal to so many of the tribes filed through his mind. Once great hunters being reduced to rum-drunk servants. Kata's question of *"Are you so sure only the Spanish are enslaving the tribes?"* And finally the words of Father Poirier that now really found meaning to the Frenchman.

*"If you really have a responsibility to these people, help them. Help them, Gabriel."*

Fortier released a sigh of relief when his decision became firm in his mind. He shrugged off the old insecurities and irresponsibility's that beckoned weakly from within and committed himself to his new position.

"Hiyen!"

Fortier looked up and noticed Kata standing beside him.

"Is something wrong?" Kata asked. "I have been standing here for some time and you seemed somewhere else."

"I am fine," Fortier answered, smiling. "Let's get some sleep, Kata. I must be prepared to face the people tomorrow. They are going to make me their Chief."

Two full seasons had passed since Fortier had become Chief of the Vermilion Band of the Ishak. The winter gatherings had been happy and uneventful and the Vermilion Band had not felt the encroachment of the white men in their lands near the great water. The band's number had swelled to near fifty and the people maintained that this was because of the reputation of their Chief. Yok, Father of Tortue, had become known for his wisdom and fairness and the plight of the Vermilion Band was good fortune.

It was early in the Fish Moon when Yok was summoned by Kinimo of the Teche Band. Word was sent that Kinimo needed the assistance and advice of Yok and could he please visit the village of Kinimo. Yok set out accompanied by Kata and Escanimon. The toddling Tortue remained with his second mother of sorts, Patassa.

When the trio reached the village of the Teche Band they were met by Kinimo and he promptly explained his request. It seemed the French had constructed a trading post on the eastern boundary of his lands and some Cannouche had visited his village asking to buy some of his lands.

The concept of buying lands seemed ridiculous to Kinimo and he was sure he must have misunderstood the Cannouche.

Yok did his best to explain this practice of the white men of owning land and Kinimo found this quite amusing. The lands the Teche Band occupied stretched from the bayou they located their villages on to the bayou the Vermilion Band lived on and Kinimo said he would sell all of it to the Cannouche if they wished.

When Yok inquired as to where the Teche Band would live, the Chief became morose. He explained of how his band's numbers had dwindled and of how it was becoming increasingly more difficult to survive with so few young hunters in his band.

Yok felt a twinge of guilt, for some of the new young members of the Vermilion Band had come from Kinimo's village.

Kinimo had decided to move south and live among the Chitima-chas. They had always been kind to his band and the Teche Band had friends and relations amongst their neighbors to the south.

Fortier and Kata accompanied the aging Kinimo to the new French post to assist him in his negotiation. When they arrived at the small settlement, they found a neat and compact cabin nestled amongst a host of huge oak trees on the bayou of the Teche Band.

The small trading post was surrounded by a number of wagons that apparently had families living in them. Yok counted twenty wag-ons and was shocked to see so many settlers here looking for home-steads. He told Kata and Kinimo to wait for him at the entrance to the trading post and he walked to where a group of men stood con-versing, by a near wagon.

On his approach, the men instructed their women to move away with the children and Yok was amused. Their language was French but it was a peculiar dialect of which Yok was not familiar. Standing before the men, he addressed one that seemed a leader.

"Good day, Sir. I am known as Yok and I am Chief of the Vermil-ion Band of the Ishak."

The men before Yok stared at him in amazement. They exchanged glances for a moment and then the man that Yok had addressed spoke.

"Forgive us. We were so sure you were an Indian. We did not mean to be rude."

"I suppose I do look like a native," Yok chuckled. "My wife insists that I keep my beard shaved. She says I look more civilized."

"I am Henri Chretien," the spokesman said. "This is Josef Pellerin, Andre Broussard, my brother-in-law Simarre Trahan and Alcee Thibaudeau. We are pleased to know you, Mister Yok."

"Where do you come from?" Yok inquired. "I am not familiar with your dialect."

"We are here from Nova Scotia," Chretien said. "We have been sent here by Governor Aubry in New Orleans. He told us there was land available here for settlement and we wish to purchase home sites. We have been waiting for the owner of the lands beyond this stream. Mister de la Claire, the master of this post told us he would he here soon. Are you perhaps this man?"

"No, not I. The man you are waiting for is standing there with my wife. I will translate for he does not know Cannouch…uh, …French."

"That will be fine," Chretien said.

"These twenty or so families will, not require so much land, I'm sure," Yok said, beckoning to Kinimo. "This bargaining should not take long."

"But sir!" Chretien exclaimed. "We are but the vanguard of our group. There are over two hundred families of Acadians enroute to this post."

"I see," Yok whispered. "In that case, let us go into the post and begin immediately."

The Acadians, as they called themselves, were friendly but shrewd. Yok did as well as he could advising Kinimo, but he still felt the elderly chief surrendered much land for the meager amounts of money and trade goods offered by the obviously poor Acadians.

Kinimo, however, was elated. He found himself a rich man by simply scratching two lines onto a piece of skin with a feather. This would really be some story to tell the Chitimachas.

Yok established a consignment arrangement with the Commandant of the post, de la Claire, for any Acadians arriving in the future. He spent a long time trying to explain this procedure to Kinimo and hoped the chief understood enough to occasionally visit the post to collect his revenues.

When the negotiations ended, they bid farewell to the immigrant families and started west for their homes. Yok wished Kinimo and his people good fortune when he, Kata and Escanimon departed their village. He knew they would not be seeing the Teche Band at the winter gathering after they merged with the populous Chitima-chas. They started for their village and once again, Yok felt a strong sense of change sweeping over his people.

As they had started late in the day, they stopped and made camp for the night enroute for home. Escanimon trapped a fine rabbit for their supper and then the three Ishak settled for sleep.

Yok and Kata lay staring at a star-filled sky and mused over the recent events.

"These settlers will soon reach our lands," Kata said softly.

"Not as soon as you may think," Yok answered. "I have been thinking on this, Kata. I have decided to move our band to the west. There is a fine river that lies between our lands and that of the Calca-sieu Band and we will move there. That will keep us away from the surge of settlers for a while."

"I know of this river," Kata said, raising herself on an elbow. It has no name that I know of."

"It will now," Yok said. "We will call this river the Nementou. We will be known as the Nementou Band of the Ishak."

"This is a good thing, Hiyen," Kata said in a voice choked with emotion.

When the lovers became aware of the steady, low snores from Escanimon, they joined quietly under their robe. When the shudders of their passion had subsided, they lay contentedly enjoying the cool night-breeze.

"Lets hurry home in the morning," Yok whispered. "I miss Tor-tue."

Kate smiled in answer.

"He looks so like Chaoui," Yok continued. It will not be long before he becomes a great hunter for I am sure he will be just like his father."

"I hope he is like both of his fathers," Kata sighed.

"Doesn't this remind you of the trip to Cata-Oula?" Yok asked. "It seems so long ago for it was such a trip of discovery for me. It was such a happy time and yet there is so much pain in remembering."

"We are happy, but we will always be touched by sadness, Hiyen," Kata said. "But it is easier bearing that sadness together."

After a long pause in their conversation, Yok spoke gently.

"Perhaps you and I could make a visit to Cata-Oula before we move the village."

"That will not be necessary," Kata mumbled sleepily. "Your child will come during the Strawberry Moon."

Yok felt the tears move slowly down his face. He rose moments later when he heard Kata's even breathing of sleep. He walked to the edge of the bluff their camp was located on and gazed across the moonlit prairie.

His future would not be easy, he knew. Caring for two children, finding refuge for his people that would keep them safe from the dangers of disease and corruption, and trying to preserve the Ishak way of life. It was indeed a formidable task, but if it was possible, he would find a way. He would keep the promise to himself and do as Father Poirier had suggested and help these people; his people. For no matter how much he managed to help them, he would never be able to repay what they had done for him.

## The End

# Historical Note

During the late 1700's, the then acting governor of the Louisiana Territory sent a government agent into the interior of Louisiana to estimate the population of various Indian tribes. This agent learned and reported that the population of the tribe, Attakapa, was approximately 360 men, women and children. Half of this number lived in a large village situated on a central Louisiana lake. The information was given to the agent by the Chief of this village. The agent reported that this same Chief was a French speaking white man of unknown origin.

# About the Author

Ed Blanchard has spent most of his adult life as an executive in the television broadcasting business. An avid outdoorsman, U.S. Military Veteran and perennial history enthusiast, he continues to trek the South Louisiana trails of *Path Of The Chief*. He and his wife, Bonita have two children and live in Carencro, Louisiana.

0-595-26025-X

Made in the USA
San Bernardino, CA
24 February 2014